TIME OF DISCOVERING

Stories of Girls Who Found Clues to Careers

SELECTED BY

HELEN FERRIS

FRANKLIN WATTS, INC.

575 Lexington Avenue, New York 22

ACKNOWLEDGMENTS

The editor and the publisher have made every effort to trace the ownership of all material contained herein. It is their belief that the necessary permissions from publishers, authors, and authorized agents have been obtained in all cases. In the event of any question arising as to the use of any material, the editor and publisher, while expressing regret for any error unconsciously made, will be pleased to make the necessary correction in future editions of this book.

Thanks are due the following authors, publishers, publications, and agents for permission to use the material indicated.

"The Pastel Twin," by Esther Melbourne Knox, from *The American Girl*. Reprinted by permission of *The American Girl*, a magazine for all girls published by the Girl Scouts of the U.S.A.

"Portrait of Mr. Cinnamon," by Isabel Kilcrin, from *Seventeen*, June 1956. Copyright © 1956 by Isabel Kilcrin. Reprinted by permission of Ann Elmo Agency, Inc.

"Too Tall," by Margery Sharp, from *Woman's Day*, August 1960. Copyright © 1960 by Margery Sharp. Reprinted by permission of Blanche C. Gregory, Authors' Representative.

"The Fallen Star," by Sylvie Schuman, from *Seventeen*, March 1951. Copyright 1951 by Sylvie Schuman. Reprinted by permission of the author.

"Fire Break," by Skulda V. Baner, from *The American Girl*, August 1959. Copyright © 1959 by Skulda V. Baner. Reprinted by permission of *The American Girl*, a magazine for all girls published by the Girl Scouts of the U.S.A.

"Merry Christmas, Jeanie," by Claire Jones, from *The American Girl*, December 1959. Copyright © 1959 by Claire Jones. Reprinted by permission of *The American Girl*, a magazine for all girls published by the Girl Scouts of the U.S.A.

"From Six to Midnight," by J.P. Follinsbee, from *Senior Prom*, November 1950. Copyright 1950 by Parents' Institute, Inc. Courtesy of Parents' Institute, Inc.

"The Brave in Heart," by Sylvie Schuman, from *Senior Prom*, April 1950. Copyright 1950 by Parents' Institute, Inc. Courtesy of Parents' Institute, Inc.

"A Night Filled with Music," by D.V.S. Jackson, from *Seventeen*, March 1952. Copyright 1952 by D.V.S. Jackson. Reprinted by permission of Constance Smith Associates.

"One Fainting Robin," by Dorothy Witton, from *The American Girl*, May 1955. Copyright © 1955 by Dorothy Witton. Reprinted by permission of *The American Girl*, a magazine for all girls published by the Girl Scouts of the U.S.A.

"Passing for Herself," by Isabel Kilcrin, from *Seventeen*, June 1956. Copyright © 1956 by Isabel Kilcrin. Reprinted by permission of Ann Elmo Agency, Inc.

"Something to Offer," by Sylvie Schuman, from *Seventeen*, January 1950. Copyright 1950 by Sylvie Schuman. Reprinted by permission of the author.

"After the Ball," by Samson Raphaelson, first published under the title "The First Affair" in *The Saturday Evening Post*, February 8, 1958. Copyright © 1958 by Samson Raphaelson. Reprinted by permission of the author.

"The Final Question," by J.P. Follinsbee, from *Senior Prom*, Copyright 1950 by Parents' Institute, Inc. Courtesy Parents' Institute, Inc.

IN APPRECIATION

I AM deeply grateful to Helen M. Sattley, Director of the Library Division, Board of Education of the City of New York, for her interest in my plan for *Time of Discovering*, and her encouragement that I complete the collection of stories here. It was she who introduced me to Cecelia L. Sarasohn, Consultant in the Bureau of Educational and Vocational Guidance of the New York Board of Education. Miss Sarasohn generously shared with me her experience in introducing stories of this kind to her teen-agers.

I am indebted to my staff at the Junior Literary Guild for their reading of the many story possibilities and for their suggestions for the book's final contents—to Ann Durell, my successor as Editor-in-Chief of the Junior Guild, and to Frances De Armand, Therese Doumenjou, Rose Engle, Ruth Clement Hoyer, and Barbara A. Huff; to Marjorie Vetter, Fiction Editor of *The American Girl*; and to my editor at Franklin Watts, Inc., Elizabeth F. Abell, whose fine judgment and understanding are an inseparable part of this book.

And my continuing appreciation is with my teen-age consultants in North Salem, New York—Karen Mortensen, Katharine Nichols, and Susan Jeanne Schurmacher, who helped me select the stories in this book.

H.F.

Looking for Clues

THE TEENS are a time of discovering yourself. Up until now you have not bothered much about the kind of person you are. But now you are wondering a great deal about it. And among the questions to which you are trying to find the answers is what you should do when you finish high school or preparatory school. Should you take some special kind of training? If so, what? Or if you are going to work as soon as you have your diploma, what kind of job should you look for? It is fortunate that you have plenty of time for answering these questions, and to look for clues in yourself and what happens to you.

One kind of clue is to be found in what you naturally enjoy and already know you can do well. Perhaps this is drawing or painting. Perhaps it is playing the piano or the violin, or singing. Should you therefore decide to become a professional artist or musician? Such questions, too, can wait for the answering. And if in the end you come to the conclusion that your natural ability is not great enough for you to become an outstanding artist or performer, there are other openings for this special talent of yours. That is what Wilma, one of the girls whose story is in this book, discovered through her high school orchestra. Her love of music and her knowledge of it pointed the way to something beside being a star performer.

But what you enjoy and do well may be quite different from drawing or playing a musical instrument. Yet it is a talent, nevertheless. Having a good time when you do your baby-sitting or look after your small brothers and sisters means that you get along well with little children—and that is a clue. When Jeanie discovered this about herself, it made a difference in her plans.

Ellen's discovery was also different. She loved to plant flowers and help them to grow. But until Sutton Craig gave her the idea, she had not thought of her experimenting as anything but a delightful hobby. Viola, too, had a hobby that led her to an unforeseen dream for the years ahead.

The way in which you meet what happens to you can bring an unexpected clue. When Valery, who was a star athlete, had the accident which meant that she could never again take part in sports, she was surprised that what she had considered a tragedy opened up a new and challenging possibility to her. Even a natural handicap can sometimes spell opportunity. Mary's height, which barred her from a career in her beloved ballet, became instead an asset to her.

All the girls in this book made welcome discoveries such as these about themselves, and so found clues for their next steps.

HELEN FERRIS

Contents

The Secret

HELEN GREGUTT

MRS. WALLACE flicked an adventuresome ant from her skirt as she pushed back her chair to escape the hot sun of late summer. Mrs. Wallace sighed inwardly. How nice it would be if she could just sit idly on the flagstone terrace, admiring the last blooms in her garden! Guiltily, she concentrated her attention again on what Dorothy was saying. After all, it wasn't every day that one's firstborn made wedding plans.

"You're sure you'll be satisfied with the bronze color, Janet?" Dorothy was admonishing her younger sister. "We won't be able to change our minds again."

"It'll be dreamy," Janet sighed ecstatically. "And I'll be able to wear it to the Homecoming Dance later." Janet looked forward to her first year in college as a series of dances, games, and parties, with attendance at class only incidental.

"Well, then," Dorothy proceeded briskly, making notes, "that leaves the green for Lisa, which is okay because green becomes her."

As though the mention of her name had summoned her, Lisa Wallace's tall figure came around the other side of the house. Mrs. Wallace's face lost its absent-minded expression and looked only puzzled as she watched Lisa's progress down the path of the garden.

"You know," Dorothy said unexpectedly, "for a while Lisa worried me. I was afraid she was going to look like Plain Jane at the wedding, no matter how pretty we made the bridesmaids' dresses. But now . . . I wonder what's happened to her?"

Mrs. Wallace started. So Dorothy had noticed the change too! Then it wasn't only imagination or wishful thinking. Dorothy wasn't given to subtleties.

Lisa paused by a flower bed and bent with unsuspected grace to one of the blooms. An unreasoning fancy seized her mother. Lisa was like a butterfly among the flowers . . . a new butterfly, just emerged from the chrysalis. No one must be allowed to pin down the delicate wings for examination.

Mrs. Wallace experienced a sudden desire to shout to her youngest daughter, "Fly, Lisa, fly. Don't loiter in the garden or they'll get you." Then she had to smile at her own nonsense. It was the kind of nonsense that would irritate Dorothy, baffle Mr. Wallace, go over Janet's head. But Mrs. Wallace knew Lisa would understand— providing she could ever speak her thoughts to her youngest daughter.

"She's different, all right," Janet chimed in lazily.

"Girls Lisa's age change while you look at them." Mrs. Wallace tried to put them off.

Dorothy shook her head sagely. "She hasn't changed the way I did—or Janet."

No, she hasn't, Mrs. Wallace agreed silently. She had

seen Dorothy and Janet through the usual stages. Dorothy changing her hairdo every day; Janet experimenting with make-up and styles. But it wasn't that way with Lisa. Lisa's soft brown hair still fell simply. Her olive complexion was brightened only by the same light lipstick she had worn for several years. Shirtwaist dress. Sandals. No, Lisa hadn't discovered glamour Dorothy and Janet's way. Lisa had lighted up from inside.

Mrs. Wallace thought she had known and understood Lisa so well—up to now. There wasn't much to know or understand about Dorothy and Janet. They were pretty and they were popular and they lived in a secure world of dates and dresses. In her heart, Mrs. Wallace felt Lisa was her child in a special way, but she had kept it in her heart lest Dorothy and Janet be hurt by her preference.

"I have it," Dorothy decided. "Lisa has a romance."

"Nonsense," Mrs. Wallace retorted. Unconsciously, however, she straightened in her chair, leaning forward as though to see her daughter better. Dorothy and Janet had had crushes one on the heels of the other, but Lisa . . .

"Love's better than a face-lifting," Dorothy smirked.

Janet said with her devastating frankness, "I thought Lisa was going to have a long wait for a guy."

Mrs. Wallace winced away from Janet's words. "Lisa's never been interested in boys." But she knew what she meant was that boys weren't interested in Lisa. And Dorothy and Janet had been unconsciously cruel in pointing it up.

Dorothy crowed, "Well, will you just look at that now!"

Mrs. Wallace looked. Lisa had left the flower bed and started toward the fieldstone fence separating the garden from the road. She held herself with the poise that was new to her and that made her body look slender and shapely instead of awkward as it had always seemed. At the gate, Timothy Wayne waited. Even from the terrace you could see how eagerly he held open the gate for Lisa and how he smiled down at her.

"I was right," Dorothy announced triumphantly. Satisfied that that was settled, she turned her attention back to the wedding preparations.

Mrs. Wallace didn't answer. Maybe it was best to let Dorothy think she was right. Lisa was no longer a caterpillar, with all her loveliness locked up within her. That was what really counted. How she had achieved it was Lisa's secret. But it hadn't been through Timothy. He was too new in Lisa's life. The change in her had started a few months ago —so subtly that neither Dorothy nor Janet had noted it— shortly after the end of the school term. . . .

Lisa Wallace progressed down the school corridor, head down, shoulder hunched. No matter how she hurried, she couldn't escape the snatches of conversation from groups of eagerly chattering girls. The refrain was all the same. Dance tonight. . . . Dance. No matter how she kept her eyes straight forward, she couldn't shut out the flaunting gaiety of the wall posters that proclaimed Dance tonight— Dance.

Last dance of the school year and Lisa Wallace was dateless, just as she had been dateless for all the others. You couldn't hurry away from that thought, Lisa was reflecting, as she turned the corner and bumped squarely into her English teacher.

"Miss Crosby, I'm sorry!" Lisa stammered

Miss Crosby's blue eyes twinkled. "I was hoping I'd bump into you, Lisa. But not quite so literally!"

Lisa had to smile back. She felt herself relaxing inside, as she always did with Miss Crosby.

"Can you walk along with me a few minutes?" Miss Crosby asked. "I'd like to discuss something with you."

A flush of pleasure warmed Lisa's face. Miss Crosby, by her tone and her expression, could let you know that she thought highly of you. It was part of the reason Lisa had written for Junior English the composition and stories that she had never dared put down before.

"My brother is staying with me this summer," Miss Crosby explained. "He's a reporter and he's been working on a book he hopes to complete during the coming months. But he needs someone to help him."

Lisa felt a stir of interest. A reporter! That was one of the secret dreams she had pushed back, fearing that she could never succeed.

"I thought," Miss Crosby finished, "that you might find working with him profitable in several ways. That is, unless you'll be busy this summer doing something else."

Lisa almost laughed. Summers were the worst, with their days that dragged. Dorothy and Janet had wonderful summers, filled with dates and parties. Lisa always felt lonelier by contrast.

"I'll have to ask my parents," she told Miss Crosby.

"Good. Come to tea tomorrow. My brother will be there and you can discuss it. But," she laughed, "I give you fair warning, Jim's a prima donna about his work."

All the way home, Lisa planned excitedly, but when she arrived it was impossible to broach the subject. Janet was going to the dance and Dorothy was going to one of the engagement parties everybody was giving for her. Dinner was early to give them plenty of time to dress. The house was full of their activities. Janet was in the kitchen, pressing out the skirt of her gown. Dorothy was in the bathroom, pinning up her blonde hair in curls so that when she took her bath they would be steamed into place. All through dinner the two of them monopolized the conversation.

"I hope I can act convincingly surprised," Dorothy said cheerfully. She wasn't supposed to know about the party tonight, but her fiancé had warned her. Dorothy hated to be surprised if she wasn't dressed for it.

"I'll be surprised if that orchestra has any rhythm," Janet

grumbled, but you could tell it was just part of Janet's act of being very blasé about anything connected with high school, now that she was practically a coed!

Lisa ate in silence. Her own news seemed to have dwindled to unimportance. As she helped her sisters to dress, she fought against the twinges of jealousy that gnawed at her, and then she felt like a dog in the manger when Janet offered her the loan of her new red topper and Dorothy urged her to use her favorite cologne any time. Lisa knew they felt sorry for her, and it only made matters worse. Finally Janet was gone, her evening gown swirling above silver sandals and the corsage her date had brought pinned in her hair. Dorothy left too with her fiancé and there was no more need to pretend. Lisa wanted to retreat to her room and be miserable alone, but the thought of Miss Crosby stayed her.

"Do you think it's a good idea to work during your vacation?" Dad demurred when she explained. "We can't afford camp for you, but I think you should get all the outdoors you can while you can."

"I'd only be working half days," Lisa said, but Dad's words made her feel like a child and she felt herself retreating from the idea of the job.

"Do you think you'd enjoy the work?" Mrs. Wallace interrupted.

"It'll be something to do," Lisa answered, avoiding her mother's eyes because they held more understanding than she could bear.

"Go ahead then," Mrs. Wallace said quietly.

So the next afternoon Lisa walked slowly along the River Road. Already she feared the job. She had never worked. She wasn't easy with people, and Miss Crosby had said her brother was a prima donna. Lisa reached the end of the River Road. Now it branched off—one road to climb the hill and one road to town and the Juke Box. Janet had left the house just before she had, headed for the Juke Box with a date. Lisa would have given anything to be going to the Juke Box with a date. Janet took such invitations for granted, but why would anyone want to dance and drink malteds with Lisa Wallace at the Juke Box? Lisa knew how she looked. Tall, awkward, colorless.

Suddenly she ran, ran until her breath caught in her throat in a gasp as she reached the summit of the hill. She pushed open the Crosby's gate and walked to the porch of the old-fashioned clapboard house. For an instant, her hand hovered above the knocker.

A man opened the door. He was tall, and his clothes hung casually on his lean figure. The greying hair at his temples made contrast with the youthfulness of his face. "You must be Lisa Wallace," he said. "I'm Jim Crosby."

He took Lisa to the living room where a fire was lighted. A tea service was ready on a low table and little silver dishes held crescents of sandwiches and petits fours.

"Looks overpowering and ancestral, doesn't it?" Jim Crosby laughed.

Lisa sat stiffly behind the tea service, obeying his invitation to pour with uncertain, trembling hands. Miss Crosby did not join them, and panic filled Lisa. How could she possibly talk to this stranger?

Jim Crosby interrupted her thoughts. "My book's going to be sort of an education of a reporter," he began. "I have a rough draft of it, but it needs beating into shape and polishing."

He talked easily and at length and with the absorption of one who didn't expect an answer. Then finally, he suggested, "Maybe you'd like to read the introduction so that you'll have a better idea of what you're getting into."

Lisa accepted the sheaf of papers and began to read. At first she found it difficult to concentrate because she was too acutely conscious of Jim Crosby's presence. Gradually the words held her. When she turned the last page she looked up to catch a pleased smile on Jim Crosby's face.

"Prettiest picture in the world," he grinned at her, "is an appreciative audience!"

The grin was irresistible. He talked on, shifting restlessly from chair to fireplace. He discussed hours, pay, what the work would be like. When Miss Crosby finally arrived, Lisa realized with surprise that the tea was cold and the fire reduced to embers.

Lisa started to work as soon as school closed. At first Jim Crosby left her alone with simple assignments. It gave her a chance to accustom herself to the typewriter, the files and his manuscript. The pages he gave her were so short that she had time to retype when she made errors, and no one was around to make her nervous.

The job itself was routine, but it held fascination for Lisa. Jim Crosby had visited all the places she had imagined. He had met people who were just headline names to Lisa. He had accomplished what she only dreamed of. He had the egoism of a good-looking man with a bright mind, but he had great charm of manner, too, on occasion. Lisa's face flushed when he came into the small office and she would become uncomfortably conscious of her heart-beats. But as she grew to know him better, she found it impossible to keep him on a pedestal. Jim Crosby was absent-minded. Lisa hid her amusement when he crossed his long legs and revealed socks that didn't match. He was a chain smoker, and she was sure that without her watchful eye he would have set himself or the manuscript on fire. And he had an irritating trick of repeating instructions that he had already given twice, while he forgot to tell her something that she should have known.

Her early terror of failure wore off and, as day slipped into day, Jim Crosby gradually worked with her for ever longer periods. Pride grew in Lisa as she saw that her efforts were really contributing to his and that he came to depend on her in small ways. She made mistakes, but she caught so many of his that they laughed over them together. It was then she remembered with a start how embarrassment usually smothered her when she did something wrong. She had been working with him several weeks when one afternoon he roared at her impatiently for not doing something he had forgotten to tell her. When he stalked out of the room, Lisa wanted to go home and never return. She had failed—after all her bright hopes.

The pages he had scattered on the desk in his irritation held her. It's himself he's roaring at, Lisa realized with a flash of insight. He's impatient because the chapter isn't working out just right. She forgot her own hurt as she set to work, reading and rereading the chapter in search for some clue that would help him. She was almost ready to give up when she saw it. The organization was all wrong! When at last she left, neatly clipped to Jim Crosby's desk calendar was an outline with suggested changes.

The next afternoon he greeted her as sunnily as though he had never been wrathful. "I think you've set me on the right track, Lisa," he announced enthusiastically. "You have a real feeling for style and sequence."

Lisa glowed. And from then on he worked alongside her, letting her share in the whole job. It became natural to stop work occasionally for irrelevant conversations about themselves. Lisa found herself revealing to Jim Crosby more and more of her dreams and fears. He accepted her confidences matter-of-factly.

"You ought to get all the experience you can on your school papers and magazines," he suggested once. Lisa's mind flew to Timothy Wayne, who was editor of the high school paper. How often she had imagined how it would be if he invited her to join the staff. Why hadn't she ever thought of offering her services!

Another day, when Jim Crosby was telling her of his early experiences as a copy boy, another idea flashed through her mind. She could go to the local newspaper office and work Saturdays. She could type and file and make herself useful and meanwhile she'd be picking up the feel of a real newspaper office! Now she was filled with the excitement of planning. Working with Jim Crosby was only a beginning.

At first Lisa hardly discussed the job at home. Gradually she found herself so full of the people and places and plans that were tied up with Jim Crosby and the book that she had to share them. Dinners were no longer times when she listened to Dorothy and Janet holding forth about wedding plans and college plans. Lisa Wallace had things to say that were interesting!

"Have you changed your hairdo?" Dorothy asked one night with a puzzled expression.

Lisa shook her head.

"Well, you've done something good to yourself," Janet insisted.

Lisa laughed, half-embarrassed and half-pleased. Later she examined her own reflection with wonder. It was animated and happy. It didn't look shy or colorless.

The summer was wearing away and the book progressed —sometimes swiftly, sometimes limpingly. One afternoon Jim Crosby put down the manuscript with a dissatisfied sigh.

"I'm stuck again."

"Let me take it home tonight," she cried impulsively. "Maybe I'll get an idea."

Jim Crosby's hair was rumpled and his eyes looked tired. "I don't want you working overtime on this effort," he said gruffly. "Anyway you must have lots of dates evenings."

Lisa dropped her eyes. In a way, Jim Crosby's words consoled her. He thought she was the kind of girl who would be popular . . . who would have dates. But the truth soured what consolation there was in his mistake.

"You know what?" Jim Crosby demanded abruptly. Lisa looked up to catch in his eyes an awareness that shook her.

"I think we're stale!" With one of his mercurial shifts of

mood, his eyes were sparkling. "My sister mentioned a barn dance in the next county. Let's all go."

Before she could refuse or stall, Jim Crosby went in pursuit of his sister. Miss Crosby phoned Mrs. Wallace, and through dinner Jim and his sister carried Lisa along with their gaiety. Afterward Miss Crosby assembled costumes for them.

Lisa had dreamed of dancing; of herself drifting effortlessly in the arms of a date to dream music. In reality she had never been to a dance and she had shied away from dancing with boys at informal get-togethers, sure that she would step on their toes or be clumsy and heavy. Dorothy and Janet had taught her all the steps, leading her patient miles around the living room and exhorting her to relax! Let go!

But in the big barn, while the fiddlers squeaked happily away, she polkaed and waltzed with Jim Crosby and joined in his hilarious laughter when they got tangled up in the intricate steps of a square dance. She caught a glimpse of herself once in a mirror, and it was a stranger who looked back at her. A stranger whose gaudy kerchief had slid back from tumbled hair, whose face was bright with color and whose eyes sparkled. She wished that Jim Crosby would always be here . . . and on that wish someone cut in on her.

Lisa lost step when she saw that her new partner was Timothy Wayne. For a second, embarrassment threatened, and she felt herself stiffening, but then she caught Jim Crosby's eye and she laughed instead.

"Where have you been keeping that laugh?" Timothy asked.

Lisa's mind automatically climbed on its old treadmill of searching for a bright and sparkling answer whenever a boy addressed her. She never thought of anything that suited her, and always the moment had passed disappointingly. Then she remembered Jim Crosby again. He found her interesting and he was an older man. Why worry? She laughed up at Timothy and threw herself into the rhythm of the music.

Tired as she was that night, she couldn't fall asleep for remembering how it had felt to dance, light of heart and light of foot; the thrill of being cut in on by Timothy— not once, but again and again. Timothy's surprised interest in her. . . .

The next afternoon the work went forward without a hitch. Human interest was the spark the chapter had lacked to come alive. Lisa's fingers raced over the typewriter keys to keep up with Jim Crosby's voice as he dictated. She was half-way through the page before she was sure his words were intended as much for her as for the book.

"In Rome," Jim Crosby dictated, "some of the Fascist sickness infected me after a while, and I found no consolation even in the ancient buildings whose timelessness was a reminder that evil men perish, but beauty endures. So I took a holiday and I traveled south to Palermo where it was spring in February."

In Palermo, Jim Crosby had met a famous actress whose name was a legend. He had fancied himself a little in love with her—or maybe it was with the Sicilian city that spring had touched to magic.

"She wasn't really good-looking," Jim Crosby continued. "And I wondered how it came about that she was forever being described as a beauty and toasted for her charm. I spent hours studying her to discover her secret. And I had to keep reminding myself that she was actually almost plain. You see, she kept creating that illusion of beauty! And then one night I discovered the secret. I saw her next to a countess, who was a natural beauty, and the mystery was solved. My plain actress moved with the grace and assurance of a beauty, but, more than that, she gave such generous glimpses of her warm, fine self that the countess looked molded in stone by contrast."

Jim Crosby fell silent. The tapping of the keys punctuated the silence as Lisa finished typing his words. She sat on the edge of the chair then, reading and rereading the words. And her heart felt big inside her because she knew she was learning a secret. Only once she looked up at Jim Crosby, and what he saw in her eyes must have satisfied him, because he proceeded briskly.

The leaves of the trees were growing tired and dusty when the final draft of the book was completed, and Lisa went to tea at the Crosby's for the last time.

"I'll never forget all this," Lisa said.

"Nor will I," Jim Crosby answered. "You took the sting out of working." He set down his tea cup and leaned back. "You're part of the book now too, Lisa. I'm going to make it official by putting you in the foreword."

"My name in print," Lisa said wonderingly.

"Only the beginning," he promised.

"Thank you for a wonderful summer," Lisa answered as she held out her hand in good-bye, "and thank you for the secret. . . ."

Lisa Wallace saw Timothy before he reached the gate, but she prolonged her seeming absorption with the flowers. She wanted to shout joyfully aloud because of this new confidence which she tested so triumphantly. Timothy waiting at the gate was balm on the memory of the times she had watched him walk past with only a casual "Hi" in answer to her own shy greeting.

When at last she walked to the gate, she returned his smile. It's a beautiful day, she thought as she fell in step with him, and there was a singing in her to match the day.

Timothy was talking about the re-opening of school in a few weeks, and Lisa listened intently, even as she noticed the way his black eyebrows almost seemed to grow together and how brown, intense his eyes were.

"You won't forget your promise to work with me on the paper this year?" he asked urgently.

"It will be fun, especially after my job this summer," she said.

"You're almost sorry your job's ended, aren't you?" Timothy asked.

Lisa nodded. "I'm looking forward to being a senior." And to making up for all the other years, she thought.

They had reached the end of the River Road. Now it branched off—one road to the town and the Juke Box and one road to climb the hill. Just for a second, Lisa's glance traveled up the hill. It would be a long time before she really understood all that she had learned from working with Jim Crosby. But she had done a job and done it well. She had new interests and she could look out upon people and see them instead of their reflection of herself.

"I am the secret," Lisa thought. Jim Crosby had taught her that and Jim Crosby was leaving today. She experienced a fleeting sadness. Then she turned back to Timothy and her smile was radiant. Today Lisa Wallace would walk into the Juke Box with Timothy Wayne.

The Pastel Twin

ESTHER MELBOURNE KNOX

HERE's my orange one." Ellen Sedgwick spoke to her twin from one of the beds that stood in their sunny room. Her gray eyes, under the roll of her ash-blond hair, were remote.

"It's brand new! You've only worn it a couple of times!" protested Bink. But even as she spoke, her eager hand rattled the hangers briskly along the pole in Ellen's closet.

"My clothes seem to last forever." Ellen sat up listlessly.

"And mine are always in shreds," grinned Bink as she looked with sparkling eyes at the gay dress with its large, impudent wooden buttons. "Why, do you suppose?"

"That's easy!" A wry little smile twisted Ellen's lips. "Clothes that hang in the closet, darling, just don't wear out, that's all."

"Mine do get a bit of a whirl, don't they!" Bink pulled the dress over her head, adjusted the wide, shiny belt, and

15

turned to face her twin. "Didn't you have a tricky little beret to match this?" she asked. "And the dress needs, yes, a string of gaudy beads—the neck's pretty plain. My beads let go like a bomb all over the dance floor at the Inn last Saturday night. It was a riot to see Sam and Jamie and Sutton scramble for them! Have you—no, you haven't! Just about everything you own, you idiot, except this dress, is that queer, faded green you cling to so. Honestly, El, it's just plain dumb to be so everlastingly faithful to one color."

"The beret's in that brown hatbox. And I don't care what you say about this green—I love it." Ellen fingered a fold of her soft linen smock with fingers suddenly stubborn.

"Seems like a dirty trick, though," Bink went on, in front of the long mirror, "for me to snatch your one decent dress and wear it to town to get my job, even if you are going to be a home-body this year and won't use it much. You bought it with your own money, didn't you—that Garden Club zinnia prize check? Now I remember; you got it for the tea dance that Sutton Craig took you to!"

"Only I won the prize for my *Stokesia laevis*," corrected Ellen.

"Huh?"

"Skip it, darling—they are a kind of aster!"

"Oh!" Bink's mind was already on something else. "Do you mind if I wear this outfit tonight, too? Sutton's taking me to a movie—he doesn't have to check in at the U. until next week; isn't that luck? What do you bet," she added, inspecting the length of the skirt with a critical eye, "that he asks me up to the big dance in the spring?"

Ellen took a deep breath. How could twins be so alike—and so different! Lucky that thoughts didn't show. Her features were Bink's, yes, but with the edges pulled in too primly. Her smile was like Bink's, but it had all the jolly little quirks ironed out. Every line of Bink, even her voice, was slapped in with dash and bright color, while hers—she might as well admit it—hers was painstakingly done in dull pastels. Goodness knows, she had tried hard enough, all her life, to use Bink's technique. But it wasn't any use. Try as she might, she remained a pale copy of her vivid sister. What if Sutton Craig *had* taken her to the movies twice and seemed interested in her "laboratory"! People always saw through fakes sooner or later—and you couldn't blame them. It was natural for Sutton to prefer the real thing.

Bink came over now and perched on the edge of Ellen's bed.

"You know, El," she said, "when you had the chance you should have taken that summer business course that I took. We may get to the U. next year, and we may not—emphasis on the *not*, if you ask me!—since Dad says it all depends on the way his patients pay their bills. Country doctors never do charge enough, anyway! In the meantime—here you are, stuck in Northport for a year, and here I am, all set to land a good job as secretary to the president of a bank! What made you so stubborn, anyway?"

"Oh, I'd loathe typing and shorthand, Bink—just copying down other people's ideas." Ellen clasped her hands hard. "I have ideas of my own! I want to teach botany or something in a new way, as Sutton plans to do. Or—or—what I really want to do more than anything else in the world is to study landscape architecture!" Now she was in for it! Her cheeks flushed with a sudden delicate pink.

"As if you'd ever make a nickel that way, you lamb!" Bink's voice was severe. "This town doesn't go in for that kind of stuff. Where would you ever get a start? There isn't even a seed store here."

"No," hesitated Ellen, "but don't you think—if I were really good—"

"I do not!" Bink was crushingly positive. "It's all right to putter around with such stuff over in the vacant lot if you like, darling. But when it comes to stepping out to earn your living, you'd better think of something more practical than growing petunias and sunflowers. Well, I'm off to see what

Mother can donate to the businesswoman's cause, in the way of some good, gaudy beads!"

The door slammed, and Ellen's seldom-used dimples flashed out in spite of herself. Petunias and sunflowers!

From some dusty corner of her mind's storehouse, a snatch of an old verse she hadn't thought of in years stepped out and said itself over mechanically, like a phonograph record started in the middle:

> De sunflower ain't de daisy,
> De daisy ain't de rose.
> Why is we all so anxious
> To be sumpin else dat grows?

"That isn't quite the way it should go," puzzled Ellen. "De sunflower ain't de daisy, De—well, for goodness' sake!" She swung her slim legs over the side of the bed and stood up, her eyes wide. "Why—why—why—that's me! I'm really not like Bink at all, even if I am her twin. I wasn't born to be a sunflower—and she was!"

She began walking up and down, hands deep in the pockets of her green smock. Presently she came to an abrupt halt at the back window—the one that looked out on the vacant lot that sloped down to the brook and her secret "laboratory." "That's been my mistake, I guess—trying to be like Bink all the time, instead of being myself." There was an unfamiliar tightening about her lips as she stared out with speculative gray eyes.

Bink came home with none of her sparkle dimmed. She had the job! She was secretary to the president of the Richley Bank and Trust Company.

"There wasn't a bit of argument about the salary, either," she told Ellen gleefully as they were getting ready for bed. "I told him right out what I thought I was worth, and he said with a twinkle, 'You mean as a starter? I can see you're going places, young lady!' And I am!"

The pastel twin smiled. "Of course you're going places,

silly! Don't you always?" She added to herself, "And so am
I! My own places!" Aloud she continued, "Keep the orange
dress—I really had you in mind when I bought it, anyway."

"I haven't many calls this morning. How about coming
along just for the ride?" suggested Doctor Sedgwick, as
Ellen walked companionably with him to the garage.

It was one of those clear blue mornings when summer
seems already hand-in-hand with autumn. Ellen sniffed the
fragrance of it like a setter puppy, before she answered
regretfully, "Wish I could, Dad, but I have things on my
mind today. Come fall, time is precious to a gardener, you
know! Wait a minute. I'll get you one of my very superior
posies for your buttonhole!"

The doctor smiled as he slipped the flower into place.
"You've certainly earned some degree or other this season, daughter. The place has never looked more beautiful."

"You're not in much of a hurry, are you?" Ellen tucked
a coaxing arm in his. "I want to show you something
special."

The Sedgwicks' shabby brown-shingle house did not have
much land around it, but Ellen had planted the small space
skillfully to conceal that fact. The entrance to the doctor's
office was on Main Street, behind a neat picket fence—gay
now with early autumn flowers—while the main house door
opened on a side street. Back of the garage stretched the
large vacant lot Ellen had looked down upon from her bedroom window. There were a couple of acres of it, shaded,
damp, and unsightly. It sloped away to a weedy brook
where, in the spring, sprouted a fine crop of rank, bright
skunk cabbage. Crops even less lovely had taken furtive
possession of other overgrown spots—tin cans, old bottles, a
length of rusty stovepipe, a curly spring. It was an ugly
place. Nevertheless Ellen drew her puzzled parent firmly
toward it.

"I'll spoil my shine!" he grumbled as the briars snatched at him and water squished underfoot.

"This *is* a bad bit," admitted Ellen; "but we'll be on the path in a second."

They rounded a thick clump of straggling chokecherry, and the doctor drew in a surprised breath.

"Didn't know I'd fixed up a laboratory over here for myself, did you?" Ellen laughed out loud at his expression. "I've been working here a lot this summer."

He rubbed his eyes. Screened by the miniature jungle was a cleared space, fairylike in its beauty. The thick growth had been cut back and controlled. Overhead, swaying green willow fringes emphasized the gentle curve of the brook. Water trickled clear between sloping banks of delicate ferns, sedges, and the paler, erect leaves of hundreds of unfamiliar plants.

"What *is* this stuff, child? And why these bits of colored wool all over them? There isn't a live flower on one of them!"

Ellen dimpled with pride. "They've all gone to seed, thank goodness! These are primulas, Dad. I started this garden last autumn as an experiment. Primulas are more or less rare, especially those tall, spiky Alpine ones and the chunky Chinese kind. And delicate colors are rarer still. They're all rather hard to grow, because they need a special kind of soil treatment. So I thought I'd do some work on 'em and grow my own seed. The bits of wool are tied only on specimens whose seed I want to save. They're just about ready to fall from those fat little seed purses—and there are thousands of them!"

"Very interesting, dear," declared the doctor, casting a quick glance at his watch, "and a mighty nice way for you to amuse yourself. I'm late. Must run now. Thanks so much."

"Wait!" Ellen clutched his arm as he was about to vanish around the chokecherry trees. "Dad, will you help me? You know everybody in town. Will you get Mr. Crawford's permission for me to fix up this whole place? He hasn't paid any attention to his property for years, and it's time somebody cleaned it up. I've worked out something to—to amuse me—for a long, long time!"

That afternoon the owner of the unsightly lot sent Ellen a hearty invitation to go as far as she liked with his land, and even offered the services of a handy man, young Tony Beretti, to help with the heavy work—an offer she accepted with alacrity. Tony turned out to be a natural gardener. He had imagination, and it was plain that he and work were no strangers. He and Ellen started in at once to turn the eyesore into a spot of beauty, while the town looked on speculatively.

"You can't say I'm not on the patroness list of this big civic virtue program," grinned Bink, holding her pretty nose a few weeks later. "I bought the fertilizer, even if it was because Ellen has completely lost her mind!"

She had come home proudly with her first month's salary, peeled off a bill, and tucked it into her twin sister's hand.

"New dress for you," she had announced nonchalantly, as if a Sedgwick having cash in hand were a common occurrence.

"You're a lamb!" Ellen had been touched. "But—do you mind if I don't buy a dress?"

"What do you need any worse?" Bink had asked.

"Fertilizer—" Ellen had begun swiftly, and then she had pulled herself up short at her sister's hoot of derision. "I know it sounds funny to you," she admitted.

When the thousands of tiny seedlings were transplanted from the imposing line of flats back of the garage into their permanent places in the wide sweeps of earth that Tony and Ellen had so carefully prepared for them, it was a delight to see how sturdily they took hold.

Ellen sat back on her heels one warm October day and looked up at the Italian boy, skillfully thinning a mass of overgrown berry bushes. "We can't run the risk of frost catching them, Tony," she murmured.

Her eye wandered over the erstwhile vacant lot. The brook had been cleared and made musical with strategically placed rocks. Fern clumps had been divided and reset; good trees had been trimmed and poor ones removed. Every foot of the land had emerged into beauty, as she had known it would.

"Cover heem up, *si?* Wid what?" Tony was asking.

Ellen considered. "The books say hay, or something like that, but we'll have to use leaves—and it will take tons of them!"

"Best place, that beeg row of maples down Main," suggested the boy. "We carry leaves home in basket—*si?*"

So carry leaves they did, that week, basketful after basketful, while passers-by looked on, amused at the gardeners' earnest haste.

Ellen and Tony were still hauling leaves on Saturday, when Sutton Craig came home from the University. Ellen, pink and rumpled with exertion, an old sweater over her green smock and a bandanna knotted carelessly under her chin, was toiling in Tony's wake with a toppling basket, when Sutton's old car chugged by and came to a screeching stop.

"Hey! What's this?" he shouted cheerfully, poking his head out of the window. "A private fire, or can I help set the town a-blazin'?"

"It's private," Ellen called lightly. "We're bedding down some plants."

Sutton started up the noisy motor of his car again, turned the front wheels in to the curb, and hopped out. "You don't know how to carry a basket," he scoffed. He took her burden out of her arms and swung it high on his shoulder.

"When my arms began to ache, I thought of trying to balance it on my head," she answered. "Like the natives in—

where? You ought to know, now that you're really at the U. What's it like? Fun?"

"Fun enough!" he answered heartily. "Swell lectures. We've already started some keen experiments in lab. Pity you and Bink couldn't make it. Bink would be a wow there —she'd make the prize co-eds look like your Aunt Jenny! How is she—Bink, I mean? Still telling everybody where to head in, and getting by with it?"

Ellen nodded.

"Where do you want these? Along Doc's front fence?" They were almost in front of the house now, and Sutton turned his head with difficulty to see around the basket. As he did so, he caught sight of the newly made garden in the vacant lot.

"Hey!" he exclaimed. "What goes on here?"

"Been doing a little experimenting," Ellen explained.

"Well, I'll say! What are these things, primulas? Must be thousands of 'em!"

"I thought I'd get all the pale colors I like by experimenting a little last spring. And if it really looks as I think it will next spring, people might want to buy the seed," she told him eagerly.

Sutton's black eyes were intent, for he was majoring in botany himself. "What mixture did you use on the Alpines?" he asked.

He spent the rest of the afternoon helping Ellen and Tony bed the plants down. They hadn't much time to talk, and it was restful—the way Ellen treated him exactly as she treated Tony. Her nose was shiny, and there was a long rip in her smock where it had caught on the wire handle of one of the baskets. More than once Sutton shot a puzzled glance at her. It was funny, but today she didn't look a bit like Bink. It might be her hair, of course. She had taken off her bandanna, and he noticed that her hair was wound in a thick braid around her head, not a curl in sight. It wasn't strictly chic, and yet it suited her, somehow.

When the last load of leaves had been spread and Tony was busy stowing the baskets back of the garage, Sutton and Ellen climbed up on the fence for a moment to rest.

"What was the lecture you started to tell me about?" Ellen's voice was even and quiet, not at all like her sister's vivacious tones.

"Didn't I finish? Well, it's because you've been working me too hard! It wasn't given by one of the profs, but by a commercial horticulturist—guy named Gunnerson."

"Gunnerson's Seeds?"

"Know him?" Sutton was a bit taken aback.

"No, but I used a few of his primula seeds last year. They have good stuff, even if they don't know how to handle it."

"Yeah? I'll tell him for you if I ever see him again," grinned Sutton. "Well, he gave us quite a spiel about soil preparation. According to him—"

Ellen listened carefully. She didn't pull one of the wise-cracks for which Bink was famous. She simply hooked a quiet arm around a fence post and fixed interested gray eyes on Sutton's face. The sun sank lower, and it grew chilly. Suddenly Sutton stopped in the middle of a word.

"Galloping grasshoppers!" he exclaimed in consternation. "Why didn't you stop me? I've talked your ear off!"

Ellen waved a casual hand from her place on the fence as he swung by in his old car. "Thanks for the help," she called.

"Any time, lady!" he called back cheerfully over the back-fire of the old engine.

"Sutton Craig's home," announced Bink briskly at dinner that evening. "No, Mother, I haven't time for dessert. We're stepping out tonight with the bunch from Craigs-mere." Bink's curls, fresh from the hands of the best hair-dresser in Richley, out-glittered the gold lamé of her smart dinner blouse.

But in the middle of the next week it was to Ellen that

the mailman brought a thick envelope bearing the University stamp.

"Thought you might like to get a load of these—they're right up your alley," said Sutton's inky scrawl on the margin of the top page. "Will send along anything else I can get for you. Told the landscape prof your idea about using snow fences to keep coverage from blowing off plantings, and it went over big."

That night Ellen smiled to herself as she pored over the bulky mimeographed pages of the lecture.

All winter long Ellen's dingy red snow fences—donated by the lumber company—stood guard, zigzagging crazily but scientifically over the slopes she had so carefully planted. Before the snow came they served to break the gusty wind and the rush of the autumn rain, and when the first blanket of white covered the town, Ellen's land was evenly protected against the stinging cold.

The last week in March, with snow still lying in sodden patches under the bushes and along the snow fence, she telephoned Tony to report for garden duty again. She replaced the receiver with a hand that surprised her by trembling a little. What if, after all her planning, something had gone wrong! But there was no trace of panic in her face as she buttoned herself into an old, warm coat and hunted out her tools.

"First, we'll roll up the snow fence," she said to Tony, "and we can't *rake* the dead leaves off, you know. We might injure some of the plants."

"Take long time widout the rake." Tony shook a dubious head.

Ellen walked quickly toward the brook. A few minutes later there was a shout from the bank—a choked, rather breathless sound, but still a shout. "Come quick, Tony! They're the huskiest little brutes I've ever seen!"

The plants developed rapidly. Late one afternoon, working until chill sundown, Ellen noticed a hint of color along the stretches of massed, soft green that matched the new fringes on the willows over the brook. And the next day, the plants were actually in timid bloom. There were definite waves of mauve, delicate pink, pale apricot, sky-blue. Against the silver-green background of other budding foliage, the primulas were an arresting sight. People on foot and in cars began stopping to look and to ask questions.

Ellen forgot about being shy. She knew for certain that she no longer registered in people's minds as a pale copy of the vivid Bink. She was identified now with something wholly her own—pastel, perhaps, like the colors she loved, but new, fresh, a copy of nothing else on earth.

Perhaps this feeling gave her courage to stroll over to the fence one sunny afternoon to speak to an old gentleman who seemed to be looking at her garden with sharp, appraising eyes.

"Am I seeing things?" he asked, smiling. "Whose work is this—the doctor's?" He nodded to Dr. Sedgwick's shingle that swung from the office door.

"No," Ellen smiled back, "it's mine. I'm Ellen Sedgwick. Won't you come in and get a better view?"

"I have never seen anything like it!" declared the man when the gate had closed behind him. "Primulas in a perfect setting! Where did you buy your plants? They must have cost a fortune."

Ellen laughed. "I grew them from seed, and they cost me—let's see—exactly three dollars and eighty-four cents. That's not counting the fertilizer, of course."

"Where did you find shades like that?" The gentleman's eyes narrowed. "And who worked out the proper soil formula for you? Isn't that Alpine stock I see over there among the ferns?"

It was easy to talk to anyone who knew about such things. Ellen plunged in eagerly, telling him exactly how she had worked things out. Her cheeks were soon almost as bright as Bink's own.

The man nodded. "Did you use any of Gunnerson's seeds, by the way?" He shot the last question at her abruptly.

Ellen nodded, too. "They're good. The only trouble is they're so badly marketed. It seems a pity," she reflected, "that in a county as garden-conscious as this one, the Gunnerson people don't think it worth-while to establish a really good seed store. Do you know where I had to go for them? To a third-rate department store in Richley, and they weren't even displayed with the gardening equipment, either. Just shoved back of a bunch of yard goods."

"But—the Gunnerson catalogs!" There was protest in the man's voice. "Aren't they any good?"

"Fair," admitted Ellen, "but that attracts only one kind of customers. The ones that are—well, I guess you'd call it visual-minded." She sat down on a convenient stone. Her gray eyes rested on the long, blossoming stretches of primulas. "I've thought a lot about things like that—because, you see, I want to be a real landscape architect if I can ever get to the U. It seems to me that people who sell seeds, and people who know how to use them effectively, ought to get together more. I'd like to see experimental gardens all over, too, where people could see them and get inspiration. They could be dedicated to causes to give them more attraction, like those lovely 'Gardens of Remembrance' in England that I've read about."

She stopped to smile at her own enthusiasm. "But do forgive me. I seem to be giving a regular lecture!"

"And to a most appreciative audience," nodded the man. "I'm on my way up to the University to give a sort of lecture myself. I'm Ivor Gunnerson, of Gunnerson's Seeds."

The primula beds were still lovely a week later, when Sutton Craig came home for spring vacation. He parked his car at the curb and hung over the fence. Ellen was so busy setting out columbines along the brook that she didn't hear his whistle at first.

"Too stuck-up to speak to a guy?" he called.

She sat back on her heels. "Why, when did you get home? How does the garden look?"

Craig swung his long legs easily over the fence and stood beside her. "Honestly, Ellen, I never saw anything like it!"

"That's exactly what Mr. Gunnerson said!" Ellen's dimples flashed out.

"I heard all about it—and from old Gunnerson himself. Say—you've got dimples exactly like Bink's!"

"So I have," agreed Ellen.

"I never saw 'em before," he blurted out.

"You never looked!" Ellen was laughing at him.

"Well, I'm looking now," said Sutton Craig. "Are you going to be too busy with that new job of Gunnerson's to come up to school for the big dance in June?"

"We're going to get the shop organized first," Ellen told him, "and then part of the arrangement is that I'm to take the summer course in landscaping at the U. So—so, you see, I'll be there!"

Talking it over that night with Bink, Ellen said thoughtfully, "I suppose I'll have to be thinking of clothes. What color shall I get for the dance?"

Bink, brushing her hair, turned to look at her sister. "That's one bet I lost," she sighed. "So he asked you! You know, Ellen, you've changed, or something. Getting yourself a job and bids to dances."

"Changed? Me?" Ellen shook her head. "But you didn't answer my question, Bink. What color do you—?"

"For the dance?" Bink considered. "Chiffon would be grand on you. I look plain silly in it, but for you—yes, swirly chiffon, very soft and indefinite, and—how about that pale green you like so much?" She waved her arm in the direction of her closet. "Slip into that new thin wool of mine, the red one. It's just what you need to wear in to town tomorrow to help Mr. Gunnerson pick out the new office. It's not exactly your color, but still—"

"Do you suppose I can get the hat on over my braids?" asked Ellen, her eyes appraising the saucy red hat, half out of its box, which stood on her sister's bed.

Bink paused, consideringly. "By the way, Ellen, how do you think I'd look in braids, myself?"

Portrait of Mr. Cinnamon

ISABEL KILCRIN

THE NEWS leaked out and seeped through school: the judges who had been appointed to make the Wilton County Art Award were evenly divided in their opinions as to who should get it, three in favor of Larry Hughes for his portrait of his mother, and three in favor of my pal, Jeanie Witherspoon, for her portrait of Mr. Cinnamon.

It was common knowledge also that it was not a question of technique that was holding them up. Larry would have won hands down on technique. His painting was far more finished than Jean's and the judges were in agreement on that. But it seemed that three of them thought that there was something in Jean's rather crude portrayal of a cat that Larry's work lacked.

The award was to have been made in late April. But since the judges could not agree, a seventh judge had to be chosen, and it was the second week in May before the decision was finally made.

All we knew for some time was that there was a seventh judge. We did not know who the judge was. We were standing in the hall gabbing one day, when Larry Hughes came by and spoke to Jean.

"Know who the seventh judge is, Jean?" he asked.

"No. Who?" Jean said.

"Mr. Miller. You know, the guy who runs the art shop."

Jean's reaction was peculiar. She stuck out her hand. "Congratulations, pard!" she said. "The award is yours."

"What do you mean?" Larry said.

"Mr. Miller," Jean explained inadequately, "is not fond of cats as art subjects."

Larry studied her gravely.

"Mr. Miller probably knows more about art than all the rest of the judges put together," he said. "If anyone should do the congratulating, I think I should." He had a nice smile and he used it. But Jean was unconvinced. I didn't blame her.

Very clearly I remembered the day we had talked with Mr. Miller and exactly what he had said. It was the twentieth of March, the last day you could get your entry in for the award, so just before school closed Jean and I got ours in. Miss Andrews had not seen Jean's painting since its early stages because Jean had been working on it at home and Miss Andrews had been out sick for a long time with pneumonia.

Jean called her entry *Portrait of Mr. Cinnamon*. It was a picture of a yellow cat standing near some green bushes. When Miss Andrews saw it she looked startled for a moment. Then she backed away a little and studied it intently.

"Do you know, Jean," she said, "this is good!"

"Thank you, Miss Andrews," Jean said.

Jean and I are special pals and have been for ever so long. We are a combination like bread and butter. So when Miss Andrews complimented Jean on her work, I hopefully waited to hear her say something nice about mine, a painting I had called *Summer Afternoon.* All Miss Andrews said was, "This is yours, isn't it, Ann?" So I had to admit that it was and concede my chances of winning the award then and there. We stood around a while looking at the other entries and Larry Hughes came in carrying the portrait of his mother. It was so good that we both squealed and said, "Wonderful!" and "Marvelous!" until we sounded like the song. Then Jean left to see Mr. Anderson about the school paper.

"Meet you outside in fifteen minutes!" she said.

"I hope!" I said.

I could not get over the marvelous job Larry had done, although everybody expected he would, of course. I noticed that Larry kept staring at Jean's *Portrait of Mr. Cinnamon.*

"Who," he asked, "did that?"

"Jean," I said.

"Well, unless the judges are all crazy, there goes the award," he said.

Miss Andrews looked at him and smiled secretly, as though pleased with her thoughts.

"Ho!" I said. "Honestly, Larry, Jean and I don't think there's a picture here that can touch yours."

"I've done better, but less careful work," Larry said seriously, without sounding egotistical at all. "I doubt that Jean has ever done any painting to compare with that portrait in her whole life. It's got a terrific feeling. It's really something."

"I agree," Miss Andrews said. "But remember, Larry, there are five other high schools submitting entries. So it's not entirely settled yet." They smiled as though they understood each other very well.

I squinted hard at Jean's cat to see if I could see what they saw. What I saw was that it had changed like anything since Jean started it. It was a picture of a fat little puss that looked as though it might very well have fleas, and perhaps burdocks in its tail. It looked as though it liked nothing better in the world than to eat and, next, to purr. In fact, it was a very ordinary-looking little cat except for its color, which was rich and tawny.

"Well, it's been fun," I said, puzzled, convinced that I lacked the critical eye. "Good night, Miss Andrews. Good night, Larry," and I went out to wait for Jean.

It was warm and a feeling of spring was in the air. I sat on the steps and looked around hoping to see a robin, but did not. Jean finally came out. She had about as many books as I had, so it was with difficulty that she held out a fist full of gum to me. "Help yourself, fiend," she said, "fiend" being our warmest term of endearment. "I'm practically starving to death."

"Me, too," I said. "The things you go through to be beautiful!" Instead of eating sweets, Jean and I chewed gum. We went around looking as though we had mumps half the time, and our mothers were horrified, always telling us how awful it looked, but we were losing weight, so it seemed worth while.

"I understand," I announced, when I had the gum chewed to the speaking point, "that you're going to win the Wilton County Award, pal. Let me be the first to congratulate you."

"G'wan!" Jean said crudely. "Who told you?"

"Larry Hughes."

Jean blushed to the tips of her not so dainty ears. On cold days they always stuck out like beacons under her yellow hair. "Everybody knows Larry will win it!" she said skeptically. "He always does."

"Not this time," I said. "Because you will. Both he and Miss Andrews thought you had a good chance," I said, trying to sound bored with the whole thing.

"What'd they say?" Jean demanded.

"Larry said that, unless the judges were all crazy, you'd get the award. Miss Andrews practically agreed."

"I'm rich!" Jean said wildly. "Twenty-five bucks! What'll I do with it?"

"I was just going to ask you."

"Let me think," Jean said.

"Never mind," I said. "Where'd you ever learn to draw cats?"

"I didn't," Jean said. "You know, fiend, that's a funny thing. I never told you about Mr. Cinnamon, did I?"

"You said he was a cat you had in the country."

"That's right. But the reason I never talked about him . . ."

"Yes?"

"Was because I was nuts about him," she said flatly.

"I know," I said sympathetically. "I had a dog like that once."

"This whole business about Mr. Cinnamon is darned strange," Jean said. "We got him the last spring we were in the country. He was the cutest thing you ever saw, gold and bronze and white and, oh, you know."

All sorts of bright and lovely things flashed in my mind: chrysanthemums in the fall, fields of buttercups, daffodils in the wind, fresh butter, golden bantam corn. "I understand about the color," I said.

"As soon as I saw him I knew he was mine," Jean said. "I never saw such a cute cat face in all my life. And when he got a good look at me, he decided I was his. No one else mattered." Her voice sounded scratchy.

"You don't have to tell me about it if you don't want to," I said.

"I do!" she said. "That picture means something special to me and I want you to know what it means. I wish you could have seen his legs. They were almost square, they were so solid. As soon as you saw him you'd want to pick him up and hug him; you couldn't help it. That's the kind of a puss he was. His head was sort of square, too, and he had the queerest eyes, pale gold and sad. His eyes always looked sad. And when he yawned! You should have seen his mouth!" Jean said.

"What was so unusual about it?" I said.

"Oh, nothing, I suppose. But it looked so new, and of course it was. And shell pink, trimmed with a few milky teeth. When it came to eating, he was always a little pig. His sides would bulge out like balloons, but he'd never give up till the dish was empty. Sometimes I'd hold his milk over his head before I'd give it to him and he'd stand on his hind legs, sniffing and trying to reach up, like a little bear."

"Well, I thought he looked as though he liked to eat," I said.

"Then, somehow, he caught cold," Jean said. "He began to wheeze and he wouldn't eat. He'd sleep all day. You could hear a scratching sound when he breathed.

"I got scared, of course, when he wouldn't eat. So I treated him. I dosed him with nose drops and mentholatum, which he particularly hated, and every morning his eyes would be fast shut and I'd have to wash them out before he could see. He never scratched me, no matter what I did to him. He just purred and tried to open his eyes and find me.

"I got very fond of him during that time," Jean said. "When he got better he slept on my bed every night. He'd stay right there like a big soft yellow ball, snuggled on my feet. Every night after school when I got off the bus, he'd come down the drive to meet me and lead me home. We were good friends, all right."

"Excuse me," I said. "I want to hear the rest of the story, of course, but it looks as though Mr. Miller has changed his window today. Let's look."

Miller's Art Shop was directly across the street at that point, so we crossed over and stood in front of the window. The sun was warm on our heads and the air had the delicious thawing smell of spring.

"Say," Jean said, "have you ever noticed that in spring Mr. Miller puts fall and winter scenes in his window, and in winter just the opposite?"

"Yes," I said. "And another thing, too . . . he doesn't go much for modern art. You can tell what everything is here. Except maybe that little one in the corner."

"Oh, that's a turnip."

"I beg your pardon," someone said in a brisk, clipped voice. "That is a young lady attending her first ball."

We had not noticed that the door to the art shop was open. Mr. Miller was standing in it. He was not a big man, in fact he was quite short, but there was something fierce about him. He was extremely neat and well dressed and his face looked tired, as though he kept alive only through the exertion of a tremendous amount of will. It was a cold fierceness that he had. You just could not believe that anything about him—his shoulders, his chin, his mustache—would ever sag. The force of his will, you felt, would endure forever, and Mr. Miller would never yield to anything, no matter how tired he got.

"Good afternoon to you, young ladies," he said belatedly. "You are interested in art?"

He must know we are, I thought. He has seen us enough times goggling in the window.

"Yes," I said, "we are." Then suddenly, "Mr. Miller, do you have any pictures of cats?"

Jean blushed and Mr. Miller looked affronted. He smiled stiffly.

"You are looking in the wrong window, young lady," he said. "Art. This is an art shop. Children's books are not sold here."

"But why," I persisted, knowing Jean would like to throttle me, "shouldn't a cat be as good a subject for art as . . ." I turned toward the window, trying to wave, "eggs, apples, bottles and checkered tablecloths?"

"A good question," Mr. Miller said, his sharp eyes flicking me briskly, "and I will answer it, young lady." He, in turn, gestured toward the window. "As you have said, eggs, apples, bottles and checkered tablecloths," he said, "such things represent the simplest needs of man, of man's body. The autumn hills, the sky, the stars"—he waved toward the large canvas in the background—"represent the needs of man's spirit. But cats!" His voice was openly scornful. "Cats represent his sentimentality. That is why they are poor subjects for the outpourings of his soul. Is that clear?"

By this time Jean was the color of broiled lobster, but I kept on.

"I asked our art teacher the same question today," I said. "She said something quite different."

"So?" Mr. Miller smiled. It was as though he had expressed aloud his opinion of our art teacher. "What did your art teacher say?" he asked.

"She said," I said, trying to remember exactly what Miss Andrews had said, "that cats are as good subjects for art as anything else. Provided the person painting the cat can catch exactly what the cat means, what it is. If he can do that, a picture of a cat might even be great, Miss Andrews said."

"Interesting," Mr. Miller said, this time smiling broadly. "But what *is* a cat?" he said, dismissing us with a glance. "Good day, young ladies."

I was trying to remember what else Miss Andrews had said. She had spoken quite seriously to Larry and me for a few minutes and I had been impressed.

"Miss Andrews said," I said to Jean, who was ominously silent, "that the place of small, gentle animals on earth might be just that—to catch and hold all the love that people couldn't spend on each other, and so comfort the poor spenders. Miss Andrews is odd at times, but I like her."

"Why," demanded Jean indignantly, "didn't you come right out and tell Mr. Miller that I'd painted a cat and entered it for the County Art Award?"

"Oh, I was just ragging," I said. "I love to hear him talk. Remember that other day? I guess he's forgotten it."

"He thinks he knows everything!" Jean said.

"Maybe he does. Anyway, come on, finish your story about Mr. Cinnamon."

"Nuts!" Jean said inelegantly.

"Oh, come on!" I said. "What does it matter what Mr. Miller thinks? Personally, I like Mr. Cinnamon a lot. *I'd* vote for him," I said.

"Ahead of Larry's mother?" Jean said skeptically.

"Yes," I said, "but don't ask me why. Now, what happened to Mr. Cinnamon?"

"Nothing. He died," Jean said shortly.

"Oh, Jean!" I said.

"It was a few days after Christmas that I whistled and called him one night and he didn't come. I found him across the road in a ditch, still warm. He'd been hit in the head by a car. His tail fluffed out so big and lovely when I picked him up that it seemed as though he must still be alive, and I hoped for a while that he was, that he was just stunned and would wake up in the morning. But he didn't.

"I buried him. The ground was frozen and you couldn't dig it. So I took him up in the woods and put him under a laurel bush and put pine branches over it.

"I remember the way the sky looked. It had started to snow and the path was slippery, going back. The woods were all gray and black and I never felt so bad in all my life."

I didn't know what to say. "You didn't tell me what he did," I finally said.

"Did?"

"Yes, you said it was strange. I thought something happened."

"No," Jean said, "nothing happened. He just grew more beautiful every day, and I loved him. And I didn't forget him. I haven't yet."

"You know, Jean," I said, "when Miss Andrews told us to choose our own subjects for the award, I wondered why you picked a cat."

"That's the strange part of it," Jean said. "I never was able to draw a cat before. I couldn't do a cat and make it look like a cat. But I made up my mind that I would paint Mr. Cinnamon anyway."

"The background was good right from the start," I said. "But that cat was the worst-looking thing for the longest while."

"I know," Jean said. "Still, I could see in my mind the way it should be. I guess I did it over five times. I had to scrape off the paint twice, it got so thick. I took it home and worked on it till I was bleary-eyed."

"Was I surprised the morning you brought it in and it finally looked like a cat," I said.

"Was *I* surprised!" Jean said. "And not only a cat, a solid cat, a special cat, but *the* cat. Ann, how do you suppose I did it?"

"I don't know," I admitted.

"Well, I do," Jean said. "And it was—because of love."

"Love?" I said, not following.

"Yes," Jean said impatiently. "You know what I mean? I mean that love can't be lost in this world. One way or another it does something positive. It's a force, like the atom bomb, only different."

"Oh. But a cat?" I said.

"Love is love, no matter what you love," Jean said reasonably. "I don't believe it's ever wasted."

"You mean if you hadn't loved Mr. Cinnamon that you couldn't have painted him?"

"Yes," Jean said, "exactly. I was never able to draw anything that looked like a cat before, to say nothing of painting one. But I did it. So how was I able to do one suddenly that was good enough for a final entry for the County Award? If it wasn't love, what was it?"

I thought of the portrait of Mr. Cinnamon that Jean had done, of the absurdly cocky, self-possessed little cat with the grave, melancholy eyes. Somehow, because of love, Jean had done something that she could not have done without love. I knew it was true.

"It's a funny world!" I said.

"Yes," Jean agreed, "but it's a more solid world now, because of Mr. Cinnamon. I feel as if I'd proved something, the way you do in math. To heck with the award! I've had my satisfaction. It's real. I did it. I feel—safer," she said.

"Jean," I said, "wouldn't it be funny if you won the award?"

"Cinnamon would be in Mr. Miller's window!" Jean gasped. "But it'll never happen!"

"The poor man," Jean said. "We'd simply have to ask him if he'd taken to selling children's books."

But in spite of all we said, neither of us, at that time, seriously believed that Jean stood the ghost of a chance of winning the award.

Finally the big day came. No one knew who was going to be named until the announcement was made in assembly.

The seven judges and Mr. Anderson, our principal, sat on the stage. On one side of the platform near the front, Larry's portrait stood on an easel, and opposite it stood Mr. Cinnamon, shining like a small sun.

When we were all settled, Mr. Anderson got up and said that doubtless we all knew why we were there. Then he spoke for a period of time probably not much longer than the first ice age, but finally got around to introducing the guest speaker of the day, Mr. Albert Miller, who was to make the award.

Mr. Miller moved stiffly toward the front of the stage. He looked as fierce as a lion. His mustache bristled and his voice cut through it decisively.

"Young ladies and young gentlemen," he said, "the decision as to the presentation of the Wilton County Art Award has been most difficult to make, because of the fact that both entries tying for the honor contain so much merit in themselves. It may even be that the young person chosen to receive the award possesses less talent, actually, than the one not chosen."

"You're in," I whispered to Jean, who sat next to me.

"You want to bet?" she whispered back, giggling.

"I think you should all remember," Mr. Miller continued, "that this award concerns itself with no merits, abilities, talents or aptitudes except those found in these two works standing here before you. It may well be that somewhere among you, sitting and listening now, is the real artist, per-haps the only true artist this school will ever shelter. And it may be that his work was not even considered good enough to justify its entry in this contest, for such things happen. I hope that is clear?"

"How nice of him to think of me!" I whispered to Jean.

"So be of good heart, young artist, if you are there," Mr. Miller said, waving vaguely in a gesture that embraced all of us. "Will Miss Jean Witherspoon and Mr. Larry Hughes please come up here?"

"Oh, rats!" Jean said under her breath, getting up.

"Now," he said, when he had his victims placed where all eyes could see them, "I will tell you what happened. As you may have heard, my young friends, there has been some disagreement. Three of the judges looked at this picture" (he pointed to *Mr. Cinnamon*) "and were convinced that they saw some quality or attribute that made them think 'cat!' as soon as they looked at it. In this picture," (he pointed to Larry's mother), "they did not see the thing that would make them think 'mother!' as soon as they looked at it. They saw a fine portrait of a very nice-looking lady. Portrait, you understand. And that, you see, is the difference. In this one" (back to *Mr. Cinnamon*), "they merely thought 'cat' and never 'portrait' at all. Is that clear?"

Jean and Larry nodded.

"I, myself," Mr. Miller said, "do not approve of cats as subjects of works of art, but in this case it can't be helped; there it is and you can see it. Tell me, young lady, what exactly did you have in mind when you painted this cat?"

"Well, I . . ." Jean hesitated. "I had a cat like that once. I lost it, and I wanted to get it back, that is, I mean . . ."

"You mean you wanted to *see* it again?" Mr. Miller said, nodding briskly as she agreed.

"And you?" he said to Larry. "What had you in mind?"

"I wanted to paint a portrait of my mother," Larry said.

"Your choice of words is as excellent as your work, young man," Mr. Miller said. "You wanted to paint a portrait and you did, a very fine one, I may say. I am sure that if the young lady had only wanted to paint a portrait of a cat you, young man, would have received the award."

He bristled, cleared his throat, stood dramatically straight. "But this young lady did not want to paint a portrait," he continued. "She wanted to get back something that she had lost. You were especially fond of this cat?" he said to Jean.

"Yes," Jean said.

"It is that quality which shows in the picture," he said. "The cat itself is definitely out of proportion. The hind leg would grow so only on a monstrosity"—he pointed impatiently to Mr. Cinnamon's leg—"but," he said, "by the standards of the modern school of thought no reason suggests itself to me that even that would be considered detrimental. However," he added coolly, "we are not considering it from such standards."

He moved a little more to the front of the stage, held out his arms in a quick, fierce gesture. "Do you know, young people," he said, "about the power of love? You know about the atom bomb, television, artificial hearts, miracle drugs, but do you know about the oldest miracle of all, the miracle of love? Centuries ago it was that same power that straightened twisted limbs and made sightless eyes to see. Today it is hardly strange that it makes so small a thing as a matter of perspective negligible. And do not upset yourselves that it concerns itself with the lowly cat. Its concern has always been with the lowly, the lost, the weak, the defenseless. It is not, young lady," he said, turning, addressing Jean directly, "because of your astonishing ability as an artist that I now take pleasure in presenting to you the Wilton County Art Award." He walked over and placed a blue ribbon on Mr. Cinnamon's portrait, then turned and handed an envelope to Jean. "It is rather because of—love," he said.

If there had been any place to fall, I surely would have fallen. Not only the reason we had thought of why Jean should receive the award, but the very words!

"Because," he continued, "through the sincerity of your desire and the strength of your effort you were able in an unmistakable manner to make love visible. And that, young lady, is the rarest art there is. Is that clear?" he demanded fiercely of Jean and the rest of us.

Jean nodded, embarrassed. Everyone clapped and Larry walked over and shook hands with Jean, and Mr. Miller then shook hands with him.

Right then it seemed to me in a huge flash of disloyalty to my current gods that all the science fiction I had ever read wasn't as strange as the thing that had just happened. When it came to the mystery of the human heart or spirit, what was there, actually, to surpass it?

Truth, I thought inanely, is stranger than science fiction! It is, it is! Because of love. . . .

It was odd, but I had the curious feeling that I, myself, had won the award.

Too Tall

MARGERY SHARP

Mary Macdonald was too tall. She took after her
father's side of the family; Commander Macdonald was six-feet-four. Why couldn't she have
taken after her mother, a neat five-feet-two? Until she
entered her teens, indeed, it seemed as though she had. At
eleven she was just right, a trifle leggy, perhaps, but everyone said she'd fill out. Only she didn't fill out. She shot up.

It wouldn't have mattered if she'd wanted to be (her
brother Ian's suggestion) a policewoman or (her brother
Toby's idea, and even worse) a drum majorette. Her nice
cousin Sally suggested that she could be a model.

But what Mary wanted to be was a ballerina; and was
technically well on the way (which made it all the harder)
to becoming at least a coryphee, when Madame V., at the
end of Mary's penultimate term at a famous ballet school,
summoned her into the principal's room for a little chat.

No pupil in the school but trembled before the prospect

44

of a little chat with Madame V. Even established performers, just there to brush up their mime, trembled a little to find a note from Madame V. For the pupils it was a sheer agony of expectation, because, though Madame V. was probably going to say something scathing about one's elbows, she might also be going to say one might walk on as a page in *Swan Lake*.

Thus Mary Macdonald entered the little office shaking all over. She but glimpsed the Bakst sketches on the walls, the framed programs of Diaghilev's first season in London, a wonderful impression of Nijinski in *L'Apres-midi d'un Faune*. Mary's knees (however straight she kept them in class) were practically knocking together, as Madame V. bade her sit down.

"My dear child," said Madame V., "there is something I must tell you. I have written to your parents already. But because you yourself have shown so much talent, and such good will to work, I tell you, personally, too. You are too tall," said Madame V.

"I've tried not to be," said Mary, foolishly.

"My child, no one is blaming you! But you are not only too tall already, you are still growing. You are growing like a beanstalk!" said Madame V., compassionately but firmly. "There isn't a *danseur noble* I can think of you wouldn't overtop already, *sur les pointes*. Supposing you needed to be supported! But even among the coryphees you would be unacceptable on stage, as too tall. My dear child," said Madame V., "I know this must be a painful moment for you, as indeed it is to me; but it is my duty to tell you that for the ballet you are altogether too tall."

"Darling, does it really *matter*?" cried Mrs. Macdonald. "At any rate you've learned to move! It's such a treat having a daughter who isn't lumpish!"

Mary, who was very fond of her mother, tried to look resigned. Children try to spare their parents much more than their parents suspect. Upon Ian and Toby, however, when they came up with their suggestions of policewoman or drum majorette, her misery found vent. "How would either of you feel," demanded Mary furiously, "if you found you couldn't go into the navy? Just because you were color-blind, or something? Besides everything else, besides being too tall, I've got two of the stupidest brothers alive," cried Mary, "and I hope you both fail your next exams!"

She turned even upon her nice cousin Sally, who suggested she might become a model.

"Or clothes horse!" snapped Mary. "Of all the silly, useless careers! Are all my relations such complete idiots?"

"I only thought," said Sally mildly, "you might marry a millionaire. Lots of models do."

"Not if they're as plain as I am!" snapped Mary.

Unfortunately, there was sense in this.

No one at the ballet school had ever worried about Mary Macdonald's face, so long as her knees were straight and her elbows curved. But she really was rather plain. She had a high forehead and her father's long nose. As a blank canvas, ready for the magic of makeup, it would pass; but even Mrs. Macdonald, rejoicing in a daughter who moved well, never imagined her daughter to have a pretty face.

It was decided among the Macdonalds that Mary should learn shorthand and typing.

Mary hated the secretarial college.

She hated, impartially, all the teachers there and all the other girls. That nearly all the other girls adored ballet was simply an added irritation. They knew nothing, didn't want to know anything, of the long, arduous toil before the final perfection that enchanted them: the audience. She could have been something of a heroine had she revealed her own training and experience, but she just couldn't bear to speak of it, least of all to such outsiders, and in fact to anyone at all.

Both Commander and Mrs. Macdonald were very pleased to think she'd got over her disappointment so quickly. "She seems to have put ballet right out of her mind," said Mary's mother gladly.

"Possibly she wasn't so keen on it as we thought?" suggested the Commander.

"No, dear; she was," said Mrs. Macdonald, who knew more about her daughter, if not all. "She really *was!* Madame V. wrote to me that they'd never had a more serious pupil. But at that age," added Mrs. Macdonald comfortably, "one does get over things. Now, Mary never even seems to remember being at ballet school. She never talks about it."

But each night in bed, before she went to sleep, Mary ran through in her mind certain exercises, certain *enchainements*; and all through each day consciously kept her knees straight and her elbows curved. These were all things she could do secretly. Though she had her own portable gramophone, she never put on a ballet record. It might have given her away. Loving daughter of loving parents, and at the same time an individual, Mary Macdonald kept her heartbreak to herself.

Making no friends at the secretarial college, she had nothing to do there but work, and at the end of the year Mary came out top all around. When it came to taking her first post, she had only to pick and choose.

What disconcerted the head of the secretarial college was that Mary didn't seem to have any choice.

"But, my dear child," said the head.

Mary, who still hated being called "my dear child" by anyone except Madame V., looked unco-operative.

"My dear child," repeated the head, "you don't seem to realize what an important step it is! I can help you a great deal, and I *want* to. You're my star pupil."

(Madame V. would never have said that, thought Mary. Madame V. kept one strictly humble.)

"Can't you even tell me," persisted the head, "whether you're interested in politics, for instance, or publishing? Or

I could get you into a really good law firm. In fact, I can find you almost any sort of berth you like, you've done so well. But haven't you any choice?"

"No," said Mary Macdonald.

Naturally she hadn't any choice. All she wanted was to get back into the world of ballet, and she couldn't. She was too tall.

To the head's disappointment, she went into an insurance company. Her parents were pleased, however, because an insurance company was so safe. Also, there was a splendid Sports Club, and a Choral Group, and a Dramatic Society: all sorts of pleasant activities to benefit by in one's leisure. Mary was growing into a bit of a sobersides, thought the Macdonalds. The Sports Club, et cetera, would take her out of herself.

Mary dutifully played tennis at the Sports Club, and became the most reliable prompter the Dramatic Society had ever known. She stayed away from the Choral Group because, though she had an extremely musical ear, she hadn't any voice; and Mrs. Macdonald quite understood.

"I still think you ought to have been a model!" lamented Sally, herself now employed by a famous fashion house. "I'm sure you'd look marvelous modeling our furs! Don't you find an insurance company terribly *flat*?"

But as Mary found everything, outside ballet, equally flat, she felt she might just as well stick to insurance. She was very sensible. Sometimes she felt quite numb with being sensible. But she stuck it.

Sally wasn't the only one who tried to unsettle her. The head of the secretarial college, hating to waste a star pupil, wrote twice. But Mary, in exquisitely set-out typing, returned two polite refusals, and settled down again. She hadn't really been unsettled; she was too numb.

But she wasn't numb (or only her fingers were) when she opened the letter from Madame V.

It wasn't a typed letter, this time; Madame V.'s violet

ink arabesqued over the note paper in personal, tempera-
mental whorls.

"*My dear child,*" scrawled Madame V.,

"*Am I wrong, what are you doing, have you by any
chance become a secretary, like so many others? Though
not such good pupils as M. Macdonald! To be brief, my
other good pupil Natasha* (so Madame V. referred to the
greatest ballerina of all) *feels the need of a secretary to
complete her entourage. In my opinion it would be dogs-
body work* (Madame V. was always proud of her colloquial-
isms), *but with travel, and at least an interesting milieu.
She is now at Carrington's Hotel, and tomorrow at eleven
will be interviewing prospective dogs.* Your entrechat *was
so good, my dear child, I draw your attention to an opportunity you may care to examine, warning you at the same
time that there will be much competition. Now I go to take
the seniors,*" scrawled Madame V., "*who are all just as bad
as ever!*"

To save explanations, Mary Macdonald left home next
day at the usual time. She felt she couldn't bear to explain,
couldn't bear to see Madame V.'s letter handed about, perhaps hear her own chances discussed, perhaps even be
discouraged from making the attempt at all. Also, if nothing
came of it, as was most likely (there would be much competition!), she didn't wish to have betrayed her secret discontent. If nothing came of it, Mary felt her heart would
break again, but that was no reason for distressing her
parents.

Conscientiously, she telephoned the insurance company
from a call box. She said (in a rather shaky voice): urgent
personal reasons. But her standing was so high with the
insurance company, it was enough. "I hope nothing serious?" her immediate superior asked kindly. "I—I don't
know yet," stammered Mary Macdonald. "In any case,
don't worry," said the kind voice, "and if you need tomorrow off as well . . ."

What a kind, considerate company Mary had fallen into! She would nonetheless have seen it bankrupt in exchange for a chance to get back into the world where she truly belonged.

For what did it matter, thought Mary, that she wouldn't be dancing herself? She might never, after all, have been really good. Indeed, what her Scots blood had yearned to, in ballet, was its strict discipline, its unremitting quest after perfection. (It's what the navy is to Ian and Toby, thought Mary, something to dedicate oneself to.)

How better could she be dedicated, than in service to the prima ballerina *assoluta* of the age? On the surface, perhaps, just typing conventional answers to conventional fan mail, keeping expense accounts in order, getting railway tickets, but in deeper truth, by shouldering all petty material burdens, setting free for the world's delight the spirit of an Odette-Odile. And there'd be travel, too. Opera houses in Paris and Rome, New York and Buenos Aires, with equal expectancy awaited the transit of the goddess. No wonder there was competition! "And I've only French," thought Mary suddenly. "How soon could I get up enough Spanish and Italian?" Although she knew her own powers of work, the answer was, at least a couple of months.

It's languages that are going to fail me, thought Mary desperately. Because her shorthand and her typing and her bookkeeping really couldn't be found fault with; and as to age, Madame V. appeared to think twenty sufficient. But if she couldn't speak three languages at least, what was the use of trying at all?

Mary Macdonald still tried. She still went to Carrington's, arriving shortly after ten. Even so, the little lobby guarding the famous suite was already filled, and by such competitors as made Mary's heart sink again. Composed and confident sat each one, emanating not only efficiency but sophistication; by some hazard each exactly the right

size to make up, together, a pony ballet. Mary took the last
seat, and tried to look as if she matched.

French was nothing. Across from her, ignoring her, two
applicants chatted in Italian. Another pair chatted in Spanish. ("Of course I speak Russian," someone murmured
casually.) Mary held her tongue—it was the best she could
do—and waited.

Precisely at eleven, a further door opened: one after another each candidate was summoned within. Each returned,
Mary noted, wearing an identical air of confidence; it
seemed as though the goddess was finding it difficult to
choose, and no wonder.

At last, it was Mary's turn. By this time she felt it was
a mere formality, a mere paying of respects. She was still
glad of the opportunity to do so; to show gratitude for such
beauty as the great ballerina continually revealed.

She was very small, was the great ballerina, much smaller
than she looked on the stage. Sitting up in the huge up-
holstered bed, sipping at a big glass of milk, how small the
great ballerina looked! But small as a hummingbird is, or a
dragonfly; ready as each to dart into beautiful motion. Mary
stood in the doorway, feeling like a clumsy giantess.

"And have *you* all the high speeds, too?" sighed a very
small voice.

A little old woman who looked like a dresser popped
apparently out of a wardrobe. "Must I remind Madame
again to ask their names?" she snapped crossly.

"I'm Mary Macdonald," said Mary.

"Be quiet, Helene," said the ballerina. "You make me
forget my steps. The first thing is the speeds!"

"Mine—mine really are top," stammered Mary.

"And you can keep accounts?"

Mary nodded.

"And buy railway tickets in three languages?"

Mary swallowed.

"Only two," said Mary, and added honestly, "counting English." It was only natural that the ballerina laughed!

"But I learn very fast," pleaded Mary. "I'm a very quick worker."

"So Madame V. tells me, Miss Macdonald," said the ballerina, unexpectedly. "All the same, even my old Helene here . . . *how* many languages do you speak, Helene?"

"Five, Madame," said the dresser.

Mary shot her a desperate, pleading glance. If only *she* would help! But the dresser refused to meet her eye. In wild imagination Mary saw herself offering a purse of gold to buy the old woman's good will. But all she had on her was fourteen and ninepence.

"May I remind Madame that Madame has a matinee?" added the dresser, pointedly. "If this young lady is the last . . ."

"Are you?" sighed the ballerina.

Mary nodded. Her disappointment, however irrational, was so great that she couldn't trust herself to speak. Then, again, she swallowed hard, and at least proved she knew what a matinee meant.

"It was very kind of you to see me," said Mary Macdonald, formally, "especially as I've taken ten minutes off your rest."

She got out of the room she didn't quite know how, probably with her knees knocking. If she waited outside in the lobby, it was just to see which sophisticated, multilingual, top-speed competitor would finally be picked. It seemed to be the general attitude. Out of a dozen, obviously only one could win the prize; but the whole pony ballet, however low this one or that must have assessed her personal chance, waited to see *which*. (Mary's own guess was the Russian speaker, who sat with modest confidence checking the visas in her passport.) A subdued multilingual murmur filled the lobby with the hum of a multilingual beehive, while within the queen bee meditated.

Mary Macdonald hadn't anyone to murmur with. She just waited to see *which*, before going back to the company.

At last the inner door reopened. At last, old Helene put out her head. "Miss Macdonald!" called old Helene. "Miss Macdonald, please to come in, all the rest to go away!"

Incredulous with joy, Mary stood once again at the foot of the huge bed. The goddess hadn't even finished her big glass of milk. With a most charming gesture, however, of her free hand, she pushed across the quilt a bundle of letters and bills and travel schedules. "All headaches for my new secretary!" The ballerina smiled.

"But haven't you forgotten," cried Mary anxiously, "I've only French?"

"*I* can teach Mademoiselle all she needs!" old Helene said, and smiled.

"Oh, I'll work!" promised Mary breathlessly. "You don't know how I can work! But why *me*?"

"My dear, you are so tall!" sighed the great ballerina. "We have just been agreeing, my old Helene and I, how easily we could pick you out on a railway platform! Of course, Madame V. has also given you a very good character; and you understand about ballet. Didn't you perceive, just now, how I needed to rest? And it seems you have the speeds as well. But the chief thing," said the great ballerina happily, "is that you are so *tall*."

Fire Break

SKULDA V. BANER

"THE INTERRUPTION will be for only a few minutes!" Miss Lib was speaking on the telephone. "Don't worry about your roast! Our men out there—"

Across the room, Maja was typing letters from her shorthand notes. Roast, she thought grimly. It was either a roast or a cake or Mrs. Johnson's vacuum cleaner! Every day since the outbreak of the big forest fire raging out Upson way, linemen, groundmen, Indian fire fighters from the reservation, and everybody—even including her boss, Mr. Jerry—had been out there in the smoke and heat. Every day, all day, the telephone had rung constantly with these calls.

Maja glanced up from her notes. "You'd think folks wouldn't have time to phone!" She scowled. That pesky, insistent phone again! She reached for the instrument on her desk. "Peninsula Power and Light," she reported crisply, as she had been taught to do.

"That's the company phone from Falls station," Miss

Lib called over her shoulder, not lifting her head from the big computing machine. "One long, two short—remember?"

Maja got up reluctantly and walked to the small wooden platform, standing high on four brown insulators. She stepped up carefully, took the receiver gingerly off its jumbo-size hook. "H—hullo!" she breathed quaveringly, before she remembered that she was supposed to say "Peninsula office."

It was Mr. Jerry speaking above the noise of the fire. He wanted her to take some notes. She hitched her book into place, setting his instructions speedily into the wiggles and scratches of shorthand. Even as her ears listened and her brain dutifully recorded, part of her mind was occupied with other thoughts. This instrument she was using wasn't just an ordinary safe little desk phone. Its lines followed the electric power lines hither and yon throughout the holdings of the Peninsula Power and Light Company, followed power lines with voltage so high it ran into the thousands! She was standing on an insulated platform because— well, something *could* happen; wires *could* cross!

"Oh, and Maja," came Mr. Jerry's husky voice, "get one of the men to take the pickup truck—should be in the parking lot—and go over to Mrs. Torell's shop for sandwiches and hot coffee. The men are famished. We can't allow them to fall through starvation! Understand?"

Somehow Maja said, "Yes—sir!" But she was so intent on *not* looking out of the window that she almost failed to understand what Mr. Jerry was saying, for above the frosted half of the big office windows she had caught an unexpected glimpse of the horizon before she had had time to look away. Even at such a distance, the sight made her sick inside. All the way to Upson and Pete's Landing she could see the thick, dirty-gray pall of stinging smoke. Before she could shut her wincing eyes, she could see the living finger of red flame through that smoke as it gobbled up yet another good green tree. She heard again in her mind the lecture head lineman Mike Maloney had given in the high school before school had closed for the summer. "Break the match," he had repeated. "Break the match and drown the picnic fire!" Somebody hadn't, Maja thought. And so— *this*.

"All clear there about sending us some eats?" Mr. Jerry was repeating.

"Yes, sir." Maja breathed with relief that she could at last step off the platform and away from the sight of the horror.

She laid the book on her desk and walked out to the rear door of the office, overlooking the parking lot. Only a few cars stood there, mostly belonging to office employees. She went down to look for the lot attendant. Nobody there. She walked back inside, stopping at the nearest phone to call O'Leary at the power station. What he said about trying to find a spare man for trucking sandwiches made Maja's hair curl. She called again and again, but each time it was the same. Every available man was out fighting the fire. She put down the receiver at last, standing there uncertainly. The men were hungry. She knew that. They couldn't go on without food. Yet . . . She moved slowly, as if drawn, to the parking lot door again and stood there a moment, trembling. And then her feet were moving her woodenly across the lot to the pickup truck. She hoped that the key would be gone, but it wasn't. She climbed in. For once in her life she was sorry that her granddad had taught her to drive a truck and help him during the summers on his farm. She had her license and everything.

"If only I couldn't!" she wailed inwardly. But the truck was already in motion. She drove easily, eyes grimly ahead, to the coffee shop. Mrs. Torell, business woman that she was, was ready for her. Her boy started at once to pack the paper cartons of sandwiches, the great urns of coffee, into the truck.

"They have cups." Mrs. Torell smiled into Maja's desperate eyes. "I sent out a batch yesterday." Then, sensing Maja's dread, she said, "Funny thing about us women—" She put her hand on Maja's arm. "When there's an emergency—"

Maja tried to comfort herself with that thought as she started the truck again. But there was small comfort in it when you were scared to death before anything had happened! Trying to think of other things, she drove through town and turned reluctantly onto the highway. For the first time that day she permitted herself to think about Alden Malone, former senior of Peninsula High—graduated only a year ahead of her. She actually allowed herself to see in her mind the glowing house high on the hill where Alden lived. Vividly she remembered how it had looked last week when his mother had given the farewell party so that Alden's classmates and other friends could say good-by to him before his scholarship took him off to his studies in engineering at the University of Michigan. Go ahead and think about it, Maja needled herself, as the smoke thickened. Go ahead and think that he'll be graduated and out of Michigan by the time you, Maja, are able even to start your first journalism classes—if you ever do!

It was the business about Alden, she told herself, that was stinging the tears into her eyes until they spilled down her cheeks. But she knew this was only half true. The other half was this terrifying thing closing around her. The outside wrappings of the fire—the gray, sodden rage of the smoke—were choking everything but the flames they should choke.

"I can't, I can't!" Maja cried, and nearly stopped the truck. What if she didn't get the lunch delivered to the men? They would understand there had been no spare man to drive the truck, and nobody would expect a girl . . .

"But *I* would!" something inside her said sternly to Maja. And the truck jolted on again, aiming straight for what seemed like a wall of solid smoke. Even as Maja stared, the tall black thing beside her that had been a living tree exploded with a roar into flames and crumpled out of sight in the burning, flaming wall that seemed within hand's reach. All around her there was a curious singing *boom*. Below, in the smoke, were the terrified woods creatures, running desperately and often in vain out of the reach of this demon that pursued them.

Maja was all but sobbing when she saw against the weird glow ahead of her the form of a man. At first, Maja was as sick with new terror as she was with relief. What manner of man was this? What was he doing here? She almost ground the truck to a stop again and reached for reverse. Then she realized that this was Pete's Landing where Mr. Jerry had said someone would meet the truckload of food.

"Just in time for a bunch of starving men—"

"Alden Malone! You're supposed to be on your way to Ann Arbor!"

"Maja Gran! Hey, what the dickens are *you* doing here?"

His surprise and hers came out together, in one indistinguishable jumble. But there was no time to stand and visit with the fire so near. Alden Malone got behind the wheel and bent to the job of trying to distinguish road from shoulder.

"What do you suppose the boss'll say?" he asked after a moment. "A kid like you!"

"What do you suppose the men would have done," Maja snapped back, "falling in their tracks with starvation, and not a single man to deliver food?"

"The boss'll have you fired—disobeying orders," Alden pursued doggedly. "What do you suppose a general would do to you on a battlefield? And this is as bad as one! Have you drummed out, that's what!"

"Silly," Maja slumped back in relief, shut her eyes, and let herself know that Alden, capable Alden, was in charge.

"*What* orders? Mr. Jerry said to deliver the food. Here it is."

"Got to give you credit for spunk, anyway. Quite a trip for a kid like you."

She bent forward to remind him that today she was a high school senior just as he had been only last week. But her breath was snatched away by the near miss of a tree that fell behind them. Finally the truck stopped, and Maja could look around her. And there, for all the smoke and everything, was a mirage—an open place where you could see boards set up as tables and men, indistinguishably grimy and dirty, standing around grinning, showing their relief in jokes and laughter as they saw the urns and cartons. There was a special long-drawn whistle when Maja stepped down from the truck.

I must look horrible! Maja thought, waving to them.

She caught Mr. Jerry's eyes—a different Mr. Jerry from the handsome, tailored gentleman of the office. She knew a moment of dread lest he come and scold her, question her about the stupidity of exposing herself to such danger. She knew he would have something to say back at the office, but she could tell from the glint in his eyes that it would not be too bad.

Maja helped serve the big fat sandwiches, the great mugs of hot coffee. In surprisingly short time the men had finished, and one by one dropped away with a smile and a muffled "Thanks, kid!"

"I'm chauffering you back," Alden announced. "Boss's order. You're not driving this way alone twice."

She tried to act indignant, but she could only melt into sheer relief. They were hardly a few miles down the road, crawling through smoke and fire, when Maja noticed that Alden was favoring one hand. "Your hand!" she exclaimed. "You've hurt your hand!" Alden tried to hide his badly scorched and blistered palm, but Maja insisted that he stop and let her treat it. She found the first aid kit that was always part of every company vehicle. Soon she was salving and binding the injured hand with quick, trained fingers. It must have hurt, she thought. He even grunted once!

"And now," Maja commanded, trying not to sense the heat and flame all around them, "you can't drive with that hand. I'm taking over from here on!"

Grimly she pushed him out of the wheel seat and slid in herself. When he got in again beside her, she set the truck in motion.

She was close to tears. I've never been so *scared*—flashed through her head. Even with Alden there! But Alden was silent. Maybe it was the pain of his hand. Maybe, Maja thought, it was partly because he was a little scared, too. It made her feel better.

And then suddenly ahead, the blessed lights of town! Maja sat tall in her seat. She rolled down the window, as Alden was doing.

"I'm not scared!" Maja said aloud. "I'm not scared any more!"

"Good for you!" he said. "I haven't forgotten that fire at your grandpa's farm when you were just a kid. I know what this trip must have—I'm sorry," he said apologetically.

"That's what I was thinking about all the time," Maja said. "Fire has always scared me so terribly ever since. And now—I'm still scared. But I can look it in the eye! Now I know I won't run and hide. Not any more!"

It was late the next afternoon. The last of Mr. Jerry's dictation was transcribed. Maja was staring out of the window at the gray smoke pall that was only now beginning to thin as the fire was being brought under control. But her thoughts were not on the fire or the miracle that she could actually stare into it without panic. Her mind was on Alden. He would be going away now that the need for him was over. He would be going toward the studies that would be completed before she could afford even to begin hers. He stood there in her mind's eye, torn and dirty and besmoked, grinning his Irish grin. As usual when she was moved, Maja reached for pencil and paper. Before she knew it, she was scribbling away. After a time, she sat back, amazed that she had turned out a full page of copy. She had produced it, headline and all, out of yesterday's terror—and Alden Malone.

IT SHALL NOT FAIL!
AND IT HAS NOT FAILED!

And then under the black headlines, she began the story:

"There are heroes every day in the public service business . . ."

She read on, nodding in approval at her account of the fire fighting. She had not quite finished when she heard Miss Lib's "Going my way?" Presently the two of them were on the street, homeward bound. It wasn't until she was helping with the supper dishes that Maja thought again of the fire story she had written. "Mom!" she exploded, and stood there, knowing she could do absolutely nothing about it until tomorrow. She must have left her piece of copy right in with Mr. Jerry's letters! Well, she would just have to be at the office before him tomorrow.

Next morning she flew to her desk. The folder was gone. She raced to Mr. Jerry's office. He just couldn't be back at work so early today of all days! But there he sat. And all he had to say was, "How about taking some dictation?" She sat there until noon, carefully entering in her notebook reports of what had happened at Superior Falls hydro plant.

Over her transcription that afternoon, Maja decided that she must have crumpled her fire story and thrown it into the wastebasket.

Just as she was leaving, Mr. Jerry called from his office, "That was a good story, Maja." He beckoned her to come in. "I hadn't thought about giving the public a peek at what we have been doing. Thanks for reminding me."

"My . . . my . . . story?" Maja was stuttering.

Mr. Jerry handed her an envelope. "Open it tonight at supper," he said, and went back to his delayed paper work again.

But it was before supper that Maja opened the envelope. Dad came tearing in, waving the "Globe," the daily paper, like a flag. "Look!" he exploded. "We have a journalist in our midst!" He pointed to an oblong of black-framed, white-matted print in the middle of the first page. Maja could only stand there, feeling her heart thud. From where she stood, she could see her own

IT SHALL NOT FAIL!

black and big on the page of the "Globe." They talked and exclaimed and almost forgot about supper. And then Maja remembered her envelope from Mr. Jerry. She tore it open and gasped. "Twenty-five dollars!" She sat down weakly. "A company check for twenty-five dollars and a note . . . Mr. Jerry says . . . he says . . ."

"Here, let me!" her father cried. He took the letter and began to read. "One day you'll be getting checks many times this size, Maja. For now, we pay you this small honorarium for some very good writing."

There wasn't much supper eaten that evening. While Mom and Dad talked about some mythical college where Maja could learn to be a writer, she sat dreaming.

"All that board you've been paying us since you've had a job, Maja," Dad said. "I've kept it in a separate account for you. It adds up pretty good right now! In a year—"

"A year!" she blazed, out of the sudden swift pain she felt. "It would take five years—maybe a hundred—to save enough money for the university!"

"We knew we could never manage college for you, dear," Mom said patiently. "It costs so much just to support a family. But we could help—and you have been helping yourself. With every penny you have earned and turned over to me, your account at National has grown bigger."

Maja was teary-eyed with gratitude, but deep down inside her there was a seething rebellion. Scholarships! Why, with a scholarship she could go to college next year! But she wasn't a chemist or a scientist or an engineer. Who could interest the power company in giving a scholarship to a journalism hopeful?

By morning she could stand the inner turmoil no longer. With a grim determination she got into her new blue linen. She trembled at her desk; her palms were wet; she was hot and cold and her breath was ragged. She gave Mr. Jerry just time to get settled. Then she picked up the mail she had sorted for him. Like a soldier to battle, she marched, eyes straight ahead, to the inner-office door. Mr. Jerry was beaming at her. He said in his usual kind way that he had heard plenty of applause for her article in the "Globe," both for the idea of it and the idea in it. Maja walked over to him.

"Why doesn't Peninsula Power and Light offer scholarships for journalism and school teaching as well as science?" Maja gulped out. It wasn't at all the beginning she had intended. It just tumbled out in a panic. "There are five scholarships for engineering students. But we can't all be engineers! There are lots of us who would like to go to the university to be teachers, or artists, or—writers!"

She was ready for breathless, red-faced flight. Mr. Jerry leaned back in his big swivel chair and sat there smiling. He let her finish, to the very last breathless word. He glanced up at someone behind her.

"Well, Alden?" he said. "Did you two get into cahoots about this? I'm getting the same lecture from Maja I heard from you last evening. Pretty solid stuff, too, I must concede."

"So help me," Alden denied, grinning. "So *help* me!"

Somebody offered Maja a chair. She flopped down, weak-kneed.

"It so happens I beat the two of you to the draw," Mr. Jerry grinned. "I can't say I exactly had you in mind, Maja, when I presented our board of directors with a plan for two extra company scholarships, one each for the boy and girl in our employ who showed most promise outside the scientific fields. But after your piece, Maja—" he nodded, "I wouldn't be surprised if you'd high-tail it to the University of Michigan on a company scholarship right in the tracks of our friend Alden here."

How long Maja sat there, staring wet-eyed from Mr. Jerry to Alden, she never knew. Something kept chanting in her brain, "Not five years! Next year!" She wanted to run and tell Mom, Dad. They'd know how hard she was going to work to win this first new scholarship. She wanted to hug Alden for helping, but something new and grown-up restrained her now from doing what she could have done without thinking years ago. She tried to find words. "Mr. Jerry, M—Mr. Jerry—"

But Mr. Jerry was all business now. He picked up a letter from the pile on his desk. His voice was official.

"A letter, please, Maja. A double-spaced report. To Mr. Walter J. Hodgkins, Ashland. Subject: the Upson fire . . ."

Somehow, Maja saw her pencil efficiently flying. The words curled in figures over her blue-ruled notebook. "Subject: Upson Fire . . ."

She saw smoke and tearing flames. That was yesterday. She saw herself in mortar board and gown . . .

"That's *tomorrow!*" she whispered low.

Alden lightly touched her shoulder as he went by, on his way out of the office. "Good luck!" he whispered.

She saw his mouth form another word—the familiar "kid." She saw his mouth shut without saying it.

The Fallen Star

SYLVIE SCHUMAN

SHE WAS small, with fine ash-blond hair dipping to her shoulders, and she had to stand on tiptoe to read the notice over the boy's shoulder. Beside him she looked like a Dresden doll, for he was big, with tan, woolly hair and rough-textured clothes. He anchored a final thumbtack and stood aside with exaggerated politeness to let her read. His brows climbed as he recognized her. "Wilma! Well, now I can give you a personal invitation." She half-wheeled, as though to escape. "I looked for you at the last meeting." Leonard Watt's eyes took subtle, approving inventory of her. "Not that I want to high-pressure you into it, but we do need members. Coming tomorrow?"

She scanned the notice behind him with its decorative border of music notes. She managed a vague half-promise and a smile and fled down the corridor.

Wilma Sperry forced down a lump in her throat as she took her coat from the locker. Two months at this new school . . . The thought of Leonard's invitation returned with the memory of his friendly brown eyes, the attractive bulk of his shoulders. But she couldn't—she just couldn't go back to his club. She wouldn't have anything to do with music ever again.

A raw wind whistled around the building and seemed to blow down the steps. She was aware of couples arm in arm, of laughter and chatter on the campus. Around a sleek, blue convertible was clustered a knot of girls. Another clique, Wilma thought, the tightest—the old, rich families of Winchester. Could she have imagined that the horn hooted as she walked by? It honked again and someone called, "Wilma Sperry!" As she turned, the dark-haired girl with blue eyes, sitting at the wheel of the car, smiled at her.

"I wanted to know if you're coming tonight. I didn't get the RSVP."

Wilma's brow knotted. She had never spoken to this girl before.

"I hope I got the right address," the girl went on with an airy wave of a suede-gloved hand. "I sent the invitation to the address the newspaper gave when it announced your arrival in town." As Wilma continued to look blank, she added, "Or didn't you get it?"

"I'm afraid not. . . ."

The girl gave an easy, fluting laugh. "I'm not very good at addresses or telephone numbers. Anyway, it's for tonight. We're having open house."

There was a gathering of warm expectancy in Wilma. Open house—the words conjured such a sense of cordiality. She was almost afraid to show how delighted she was. "Well . . ."

The girl stopped smiling a moment and studied her. "You *are* Wilma Sperry? Claude Sperry's daughter?"

It was as though something had struck her a blow. "Yes, I am."

"Fine. Then I'll see you tonight. About eight." She mentioned an address. "Anyone will point it out to you. By the way, I'm Marjorie Nelson. Hello and good-by." She turned the ignition key and slid smoothly away.

Claude Sperry's daughter . . . a smile hovered about Wilma's lips. She should have known it would be no different—especially in a town like Winchester, with its own conservatory . . . well-known artists performing nightly in the school auditorium. . . . Here particularly, her father's name as a great teacher would be alive. Suddenly his face rose before her, and she saw his fingers curled about the neck of the violin. It didn't seem possible that he was gone. Part of her life, so bound up with his, had died with him. How she had fought moving to Winchester, but her mother's relatives were all here. Now just what she had feared so much had come in the shape of Marjorie Nelson's invitation.

Her mother was holding the envelope with the card when she got home. "It went to the wrong address." She gave Wilma time to read it. "Aunt Laura says the Nelsons are very musical. Will you go?"

"I'm not sure." Their eyes met. Not once since her father's death had they discussed Wilma's playing. She had had the feeling her mother was waiting for something, watching and waiting. She felt gratitude toward her for not pushing the invitation.

She thought, as the afternoon wore on: Maybe I'm just sensitive. Maybe Marjorie Nelson didn't mean it that way. Finally, she took a gold velveteen dress from the closet. The color brought out the gold of her hair, the hidden amber of her eyes. All the while she dressed, she was still not sure that at the last minute she might decide not to go.

Marjorie Nelson's effusive greeting embarrassed her. With one arm tucked around Wilma's waist she guided her to the living room. "Wilma Sperry," she announced.

"You know, Claude Sperry's daughter." Wilma was conscious of eyes focusing on her as though she were a curiosity. There was a disjointed impression of the most beautiful living room she'd ever seen, and then Marjorie was saying, "My brother, Richard."

He smiled and his eyes, the same brilliant blue as Marjorie's, were intent upon her. "Claude Sperry's daughter!" he repeated with amazed satisfaction.

"You knew my father?" she asked.

"I wish I had. I'd certainly be studying with him today instead of going to the conservatory. There certainly was no greater American teacher than Claude Sperry. Why, you could count his students who became famous. But let me get you some refreshments." He was back in a moment with punch. "You're tiny," he said unexpectedly. "I almost lost you."

A feeling of hope rose in her. She felt something stirring, as though after a drugged sleep.

"You play, of course?"

"Of course." She tried to sound casual.

"Why didn't you bring your fiddle with you tonight?"

"Was I supposed to?"

He flipped his palms outward. "But everyone knows to bring his instrument when he comes to the Nelsons."

The little lie sprang to her lips before she could stop it. "My fiddle's being repaired. In New York."

"Oh!" There was disappointment in the sound. He went on brightly. "Bet it's a fine instrument."

"It is." That, at least, was genuine.

A hand clapped Richard's shoulder. "Let's make music, Rick."

"Professor Ewing, the power behind the conservatory," Richard chuckled. "You'll have to audition for him if you enter. He's an old friend of the family; that's how I made it. But you won't have any trouble. She's the daughter of Claude Sperry," he said to the professor.

The rest of the evening was a dream. The gathering brimmed with talent, and Mrs. Nelson, in a rustling dinner gown, whisked the young people from group to group.

Richard made easy conversation, drawing Wilma into the charmed circle.

Yet over her hung a shadow, as she found herself replying to some new question about her father. A sense of being an impostor here assailed her, along with a yearning to "belong." She was grateful when Richard asked to drive her home, but in the blue convertible, snug beside him, the feeling persisted.

Before her house he asked, "There's a concert tomorrow. May I pick you up for it?"

She found her hand in his. "I'd love it."

As she was going upstairs, he called, "I hope your fiddle's ready soon. We'll get a quartet together."

She went straight to her room and opened the brown leather violin case. The curved, amber instrument glowed against green baize. She ran an idle finger over it, then flung herself upon the bed, sobbing. Richard would find out. They would all find out. She saw herself as a little girl in a starched pinafore, practicing for hours; heard her father's patient reproaches, growing less patient as time went by. "No—you play without spark!" She would burst into tears, knowing she was failing him.

Through a blur of tears she studied the framed photograph of her father. She hadn't touched the violin since he died. It lay in its case, a reproach. Sorrow wound mutely through her as she undressed. She thought, I won't see Richard tomorrow. I'll call and say I can't make it. . . .

But all next day the thought of seeing him pressed in on her. She had a right to good times like other girls. At the back of her mind she assembled excuses to stall off the day when she must play for Richard. . . .

There was the usual quiet buzz in the audience before the concert. Wilma felt a little breathless. Richard knew so many people. She was walking to their seats with him when someone called to her. It was Leonard Watt.

She became aware of stiffness in Richard, noticed suddenly how steadfastly Leonard's eyes ignored him. Something made her ask, "You know each other?"

"Oh, yes," Richard said. "Watt took over the music club when I graduated." She thought there was a note of something like contempt in his voice. "I hear you're kind of bankrupt now."

Leonard looked calmly back at Richard. "We'll survive, even without you and your crowd."

Richard cupped his hand around her elbow. "Let's get to our seats." He arranged her coat over her shoulders. "Watt's a dub. They're all dubs in that bunch."

"A dub?"

"Oh, you know. Amateurs with sentimental feelings about music, but lousy musicians."

His words started an uneasiness in her. That was why she hadn't wanted to go back to the music club. It hurt to be Claude Sperry's daughter and to have no more palpable musical identity than this group—record listeners, botchy ensemble players.

Something Leonard said came back to her. "What did he mean—'We'll survive, despite you and your crowd'?"

Richard's head went back in a laugh. "Can I help it if my friends are loyal? They dropped out when Watt and others like him joined. The whole atmosphere deteriorated. Then Marjorie left and her friends followed." He took her hand as the lights lowered. "But why talk about him? We're different."

The days ahead were full of Richard. When she could forget who she was, and that Richard kept asking when her fiddle would be ready, she was buoyant, happy. But it had to be only a matter of time before Richard found out. One day he casually handed her his violin. "C'mon, play this one. I want to hear you."

As she tucked her chin into the ebony chin-rest, she thought he must surely hear the pounding of her heart. Somehow she drew the bow and, with a great effort, tossed off a few bars from a Paganini *Caprice* she couldn't play through. She set the fiddle down with a laugh. "No fair. I can't do me justice on your violin."

Later she opened her violin case. Tentatively she plucked a string. With hope fluttering in her, she started to play. She played without music, snatches and fragments coming back in floods of memory. The small bedroom was filled with sound. She heard Richard saying, "Of course, you're coming to the conservatory next term. Auditions are in March."

She couldn't go on dodging. Wilma lifted out the old music books. She fetched a metronome, set it ticking, and started earnestly to practice.

When March blew in, and the audition loomed closer, her days took on a feverish urgency, as if she were trying to compress years of work into them. At night her head ached and her limbs were dull with fatigue. . . .

"Well, well, Wilma," Professor Ewing clucked. "So the day finally arrives." She stood in a high-vaulted room. Sunlight flooded in, burnishing Ewing's spectacles and bald head. He turned to three other members of the conservatory staff. "This is Claude Sperry's daughter."

Nervousness darted at her like an adder, and she tried to cling to her mother's words: "Tell yourself this is not important; relaxation—that's the secret of playing well, your father always said."

But the words were hollow. It *was* important. Everything depended on it. Her heart pounded and her fingers seemed to lose their strength. A silent chant started in her mind: "Don't be nervous, don't be . . . you can't play well if you're nervous." But she heard the first notes coming out wavery and thin.

A week later when she opened the long white envelope

from the conservatory she knew what it held. Her fingers tore clumsily at the envelope. Her entrance rating was sixty-nine—a wretched passing mark that said, "You know enough to get into the conservatory, but we haven't much hope."

Suddenly she couldn't stay in her room with the music stand and her father's photograph on the dresser. She put on her coat and tied a scarf over her head. The night wind battered her so that it was hard to think.

Gradually the hurt dwindled to numbness, and she realized with a start that the clock tower over the school building showed eight. She had a date at Richard's house this evening. She couldn't face it, she just couldn't. She'd have her mother phone, say she was ill.

She called home from a booth in a luncheonette. "I'm just not in the mood to go," Wilma reassured her mother.

As she emerged from the luncheonette, a figure in a bulky tweed topcoat came down the steps of the school building. "What's the rush?" Leonard Watt caught up with her. "Aren't you going in the wrong direction? The concert's that-a-way."

"Concert?"

"Sure. Violet Orenesco." The name didn't connect. "A violinist," Leonard went on. "If you belonged to the music club you could get in for a quarter."

"I really couldn't. I—"

She took a step to leave, but Leonard put his hand on her arm. "I know I don't rate next to Richard Nelson, but you don't have to treat me like poison."

In the dark she made out the tautness of his jaw, and a quick sympathy for him flowed out of her own pain. "You're being silly, Leonard." She made her voice sound light. "And to prove it, I think I *will* go with you."

Over ice cream later, Leonard asked, "Have a good time?"

"Yes, I did." The words came out with emphasis. Suddenly Richard invaded her thoughts. Leonard seemed to vanish, and there was nothing but regretful yearning for Richard.

"You've run away again," Leonard said.

She forced a smile. "You're a mind reader."

"Something seems to be bothering you, Wilma. I—feel it when we're together."

"Really?" She felt tired and a bit reckless. "Maybe it's being Claude Sperry's daughter."

"Claude Sperry?" Leonard's eyes were blank.

"You mean—? But all this chasing me for the club—?"

He shrugged. "I want members, and you seemed to know music."

Her voice was unsteady. "I *really* am having a good time."

"Maybe I can persuade you to come to a party tomorrow night—some of the kids from the club."

"I'd like to." A second later she realized that Saturday nights were reserved for Richard. . . .

But Richard didn't call. She hovered at the phone, nerving herself to ring him. He'd be sure to ask about the audition. Her heart thumped so that it was hard to breathe. She stood at the phone a full five minutes, but couldn't muster the courage. She went to her room, thinking she must prepare for this party tonight, smothering her anxiety.

When she came down, she found Leonard in the foyer talking with her mother. There was a ring of cheeriness to Mrs. Sperry's voice when she said, "Enjoy yourselves."

As they turned up the walk of a house undistinguishable from the others on the block, Leonard said, "This is not in a class with the Nelson place."

A red-haired girl with a peppering of freckles opened the door. "Greetings and salutations," she said. They followed her to a rumpus room gaily decorated with banners and cartoons. A radio was playing and couples were dancing.

She felt lost at first. They were all so informal, laughing, dancing, singing and chatting loudly in groups. It was not at all like the decorum of a Nelson open house. Then without realizing it, she was laughing and chatting and gossiping with Joan, their freckled-faced hostess, so that it seemed impossible that they had only met tonight.

The next moment Joan asked surprisingly, "How about some music now? Real music, that is."

As if by instinct, Wilma backed off to a corner.

She gaped when instruments appeared and folding chairs were set up in the center of the room. Leonard sat with a viola in his hand. She had to smile. Come to think of it, Leonard was just right for a viola. Joan wiggled a cello prong into the floor. There were two violinists and a lonely clarinet. Leonard gave a beat with his foot.

It took a little time for Wilma to recognize the Mozart quintet, for the players were pulling in all directions. Finally they hit a snag.

Wilma stepped forward on impulse. She said, "Dan, you take the beat. It's up to the first violinist to lead."

Dan looked sheepish. "Not me. I'm too new at this."

The next moment she had borrowed Dan's violin and, using the bow as a baton, started them off. Then she found the place and joined in. She had to stop for corrections or play *fortissimo* to give them the rhythm. They made mistakes, but they were good-natured.

By the end of an hour, Wilma had whipped some shape into the quintet, and, when they finished, Joan cried, "You're terrific! Wilma, we need you!"

Wilma felt her cheeks glowing. Then the thought of Richard and the sixty-nine cut across her joy. Sure, here among the dubs she was terrific.

Sunday was gray and gusty, and as she lifted the phone her throat was dry. Richard's tone held a coolness that made her chatter nervously.

Something twisted inside as she asked, "Rick—is anything wrong?"

"You sound tragic," he said.

She took a breath and made her voice light. "I've got good news. I'll be at the conservatory. I've passed." There was a silence.

"Congratulations. . . . Look, Wilma, there are some things I've got to do. I'll call you."

She wanted to be alone with her unhappiness. Through the window of her room she watched the wind shaking the bare trees, and thoughts of Richard moved restlessly in her . . .

She made a point of hurrying to Marjorie's table during lunch hour.

"We had quite a time Friday night. Too bad you weren't over," Marjorie said. She paused with the air of one who has news in store. "Professor Ewing was there."

The color drained from Wilma's face, and her knuckles, pressing on the table top, showed white. Marjorie's eyes darted maliciously toward her. "We asked about your audition. We were all so *very* curious."

She wouldn't be able to stand it. "Oh, there's Joan. I must see her a moment." She ran quickly, bumping into someone, blinking back tears.

How could she ever face them, all Marjorie's crowd? She wouldn't go to the conservatory. What was the use?

In her room that night she read and moped and moped and read and waited for Richard to call. Because he would call, he had to. No one could be so cruel.

Her mother's voice caroled upstairs. "Someone to see you, Wilma." Her heart thudded, and she quickly combed her hair. She flew downstairs, coming to an awkward halt as her eyes found Leonard Watt. There was a short silence.

He asked, with that odd insight she'd noticed, "Disappointed?"

She didn't know where to look. "Why no, don't be silly."

He went on in a different tone. "The gang heard that you made the conservatory. They want to throw a party for you. . . ." She stared at him with unbelieving eyes. "And

I'm supposed to talk you into joining the club. You see, they want to put on a concert. They want you to rehearse them."

She was torn between laughing and crying. Her mother and Leonard were watching her, waiting for a reply. She knew if she said anything, she *would* cry. She turned and ran.

She lay in the darkness of her room, her thoughts spinning. The door opened and her mother came to sit beside her.

"Wilma, you're hurting yourself—punishing yourself for something that's not your fault. You're what you are. You can't be something else."

She put her head in the pillow and cried. And slow relief passed through her.

She was alone now, the tears dry on her cheeks. Her mind felt sharp and clear, and her mother's words opened into meaning. She had tried so hard to bring something from herself that wasn't there. Some had it—some like Richard. . . . She understood now why it was called a "gift," something the gods capriciously threw in or left out.

She paced the room and little pricklings of healthy anger started in her. There was no need for her to slink about in corners. Not everyone could be a Madame Curie, yet a laboratory assistant was of service, too. So, she was a dub.

She picked up her violin, noticing its amber glow in the lamplight, its worn varnish and graceful lines. I'll go to the conservatory, she thought. I'll prepare as well as I can. I don't have to be a soloist. I can teach as my father did, or play in an orchestra. And I can forget Richard Nelson— eventually—I guess. . . .

She went to the phone and dialed a number. "Hello, Leonard?" Her words came out with a rush. "I'm sorry I blew up before. I'm coming to the party. I wouldn't miss it for anything."

Merry Christmas, Jeanie

CLAIRE JONES

JEANIE tied the ends of the tinsel on the last of the halos and sighed with relief. "There," she said. "That's finished. Fifteen halos, for fifteen little imps."

Her mother, at the kitchen table, littered now with scraps of cardboard and crêpe paper, looked up with a smile. "I'm just finishing the last wing. Are you going to be in time for rehearsal?"

Jeanie glanced at the kitchen clock. "Just barely," she said. "And I'd never have made it if you hadn't helped."

She stood up and stretched. "Ooh, I'm tired. I never should have volunteered to make all these wings and halos, but the mothers looked so vague when I tried to explain how to make them."

She began to pile the halos and the little white wings in the big cardboard box on the table. "I'll need to be on time," she went on. "I was five minutes late yesterday, and, A, there had been three fights; B, somebody had torn one of

77

the hymnals in two; and C, Tommy Warren had scattered the hay from the manger *all over* the church floor. It took me an hour to sweep it up."

"Good gracious!" Her mother sounded shocked. "And Mrs. Warren seems to be such a lovely person."

"She is," Jeanie said. "And I can't help liking Tommy in spite of everything. He can be a real lamb when he wants to be. He just doesn't happen to want to very much of the time." She grinned. "I've had to resist the impulse to turn Terrible Tommy over my knee for six days. I hope I can hold out one more day. Yesterday, in addition to the hay business, he pulled the chair out from under the Angel Gabriel and locked one of the shepherds in the choir dressing room!"

As she finished tying up the box, she added thoughtfully, "I think the real trouble is that Tommy has wanted to be a Wise Man ever since the rehearsals began, but we already had three. I put him in the Heavenly Host, and he's been rebelling ever since." She grinned. "No one could accuse me of type casting in Tommy's case."

"Jeanie, honey," her mother said. "I still feel guilty about having volunteered your services to direct this pageant. But when Mrs. Thomas said at the women's meeting that they just didn't know who would do it this year, and I thought how good you are at things like this, well, I just . . ." Her voice trailed away. And then she added, "I know it's not a very exciting way to spend your Christmas holidays, rehearsing thirty little children every day."

Jeanie avoided her mother's eyes. "It's all right, Mother," she said. "I haven't minded it. I didn't have anything else to do. Besides, it will be over tonight."

She busied herself clearing the mess from the kitchen table, hoping that her mother would not guess how disappointing the pre-Christmas season had been.

She hadn't been invited to a single Christmas party. She hadn't had anyone to prowl with her through the holiday-sparkling stores. There had been no one to invite to make cookies and candy, no one with whom to giggle over Christmas plans and shopping lists.

She had been in Center City High only a few weeks—too short a time to make any friends. Her classmates hadn't been deliberately unkind. They were busy with their own plans, and she hadn't known how to make the first advances.

She had heard that it was always difficult to break into a new school. It had been terribly hard for her. She had felt shy and lonely and out of place, and had longed desperately for the familiar surroundings she and her parents had left so suddenly when Dad had been offered this new job.

She swallowed the lump which kept sticking in her throat whenever she thought of home. This new house was a part of the strangeness. This house, where the phone never rang, and where the kitchen never echoed with the noise and laughter of a crowd of young people at a Saturday night get-together.

Well, she would just have to make the best of it. Tonight was Christmas Eve. She would spend the afternoon rehearsing with the children, come home for a bite of supper, and go back to the church for the performance of the pageant. Then she and Mother and Dad would put up the tree and have the traditional cookies and hot chocolate.

If she had been back in Elmsford, there would have been a party somewhere afterward, and she of course would have been invited. Maybe they all would have gone caroling. Or there would have been a gift exchange. Perhaps the gang would have gone to a midnight service together. She felt hot tears stirring behind her eyelids.

She crammed the scraps of paper and cardboard into the big kitchen wastebasket. She turned her back to her mother so that the tears wouldn't show and said, "I'm going to run upstairs and get my coat and the script. I'll pick up the wings and halos on my way out."

Up in her room, she had to fight the impulse to throw herself on her bed and cry. There just wasn't any time for it. It wouldn't do any good, anyway. Things were the way they were, and that was all there was to it.

She knew it was hard for her mother, too. She didn't make friends easily either, and she must be lonely. Jeanie was sure the desire to become a part of this new community had been one reason she had volunteered her daughter's services as director of the children's pageant.

Jeanie opened the closet door to get her coat, and her glance fell on the new red dress. She touched the crisp taffeta wistfully. When her mother had started to make it a few weeks ago, Jeanie had hoped she would be invited to something during the holidays.

When the dress was finished and was even prettier than she had imagined it, she had kept hoping. By the last day of school, she had had to face the fact that she wouldn't wear it. Not this year, anyway.

She sighed deeply, and closed the closet door. There wasn't much time to gather up her things and get to the church. She looked at herself in the mirror and frowned. She was a mess. Dark hair pulled back in an untidy knot; a smudge on her cheek; disreputable sweater and skirt. She had had to work at top speed to get the costumes done.

There wasn't time to change now. Nobody would notice her. The five- and six-year-olds didn't care, and their harassed mothers were too busy trying to keep up with their children to notice how she looked.

She shrugged into her coat, grabbed the tattered script and dashed down the steps to the kitchen. She dropped a kiss on her mother's hair and started to the door. Her mother's voice stopped her.

"Jeanie," she said, and her voice held understanding, "I'm sorry about Christmas being so—so dull for you this year."

Jeanie managed a smile, she hoped a convincing one.

"It doesn't matter, Mother. There'll be lots of other Christmases."

It was true, she thought, as she hurried along the windswept streets. She hadn't any right to feel sorry for herself. Mother and Dad were wonderful. And there *would* be other Christmases.

But the empty, left-out feeling kept nagging at her, and the sparkling trees in the windows, the houses with lights and laughter spilling out the doors, only made it worse.

Then the bedlam of rehearsal, the attention to the dozens of details which still had to be taken care of, absorbed her, and she forgot about her troubles for the moment.

Little Susan Mitchell, who was portraying Mary, proudly displayed a tooth she had lost the night before. A front one! Jeanie groaned. "Try to remember not to smile, Susan."

The halos and wings had to be fitted. The Wise Man's box of myrrh had to be recovered forcibly from a little girl who had put her doll to sleep in it. Jeanie's head began to ache. Singly, the children were adorable. En masse, they were almost maddening.

When it came time for the Angelic Host to make its appearance, Jeanie herded the reluctant angels onto the stage, wings drooping, halos slipping. It was then that she missed Tommy. At almost the same moment, she heard loud wails from the vestibule at the back of the church, unmistakably his.

"Go on with your song, children," she said hurriedly. Tommy must have hurt himself. She rushed to the vestibule and burst through the swinging doors. A tall, blond boy had Tommy across his knees and was applying the palm of his hand to the seat of Tommy's pants.

"Stop that," Jeanie cried. "What do you think you are doing?"

The blond boy regarded her calmly. He said, over the noise of Tommy's protests, "I know what I'm doing. I'm doing what Mother ought to do more often." He gave

Tommy a last spat and set him on his feet. His cries died away to injured sobs.

The boy grinned at Jeanie. "You must be the 'wunnerful Miss Jeanie' Tommy's been talking about all week. He's been so enthusiastic, I thought maybe I ought to see for myself."

Jeanie felt her face burn. She was embarrassingly conscious of her old skirt and her rumpled hair. At the same time, she was aware of the boy's deeply blue eyes, his broad shoulders, his pleasant smile.

"I'm Cliff Warren, Tommy's brother," he said. "I really came along to see if I could give you a hand. Mother said the spotlight kept falling down yesterday, and I've been doing quite a lot of stagecraft at the University this year. I'll be glad to fix it, if I can."

Jeanie's cheeks grow hotter. "Well I—that is—thank you— I can't seem to make it stay up." She groaned inwardly. How stupid she was sounding.

Cliff smiled again. "I'll see what I can do."

An especially loud sniff from Tommy brought Jeanie's attention back to him. She said breathlessly, conscious of Cliff's blue eyes on her, "Come on, Tommy. The angels are rehearsing now, and you don't even have on your costume."

"You mean he's *not* a Wise Man?" Cliff sounded puzzled. "Then what was the idea of cutting up my bathrobe?" He picked up what was left of a red-striped robe from a chair in the vestibule and held it up. "I discovered this in the bag Tommy was carrying. I don't usually go around spanking Tommy in public places, but when I found he'd cut my one and only robe, I just couldn't restrain myself. He said he had to have it to be a Wise Man."

"Oh, dear," Jeanie said. "I've explained and explained that we already have three Wise Men. I've told him being an angel is every bit as nice, but I can't seem to convince him."

"Well, I'll convince him," Cliff said firmly. He turned to Tommy. "Now get in there with the rest of the angels, and I don't want any more trouble from you."

Tommy's lower lip trembled, but he went.

Surprisingly, the rehearsal went smoothly after Cliff came in. He anchored the spotlight firmly to a pillar. He fixed the angel's star on a pulley so that it could be worked out of sight of the audience. He separated two bickering shepherds with such authority that they did their scene better than it had ever been done. And, most remarkable of all, Tommy, in the presence of his brother's watchful eye, was subdued and quiet. Really, quite angelic.

Cliff sat down beside Jeanie in the audience when he had finished the technical jobs. Although Jeanie kept her eyes on the script and on the children on the stage, she was pleasurably conscious of his nearness. If only, she thought, I'd dressed up a little to come to rehearsal. And then she warned herself firmly, Now don't start hoping again. He's just being kind. That's all.

And then it was time for the Wise Men's scene. The three little boys, dressed in bathrobes and draped in Turkish towels, with cardboard crowns perched rakishly on their heads, marched importantly down the aisle, singing lustly, "We Three Kings of Orient Are," in slightly off-key treble voices.

Jeanie saw Tommy standing at one side of the stage watching the Wise Men, his expression longing, his eyes wistful.

With a sudden flash of understanding, she thought, he wants to be a Wise Man so very much. He wants it as much as I wanted something wonderful to happen for me. He's yearning for just a very little miracle.

On impulse, she called him to her. "Tommy," she said, "I think what this pageant needs is another Wise Man. Particularly one in this bright red robe. Go put it on, and you may rehearse this scene with the others."

Tommy's eyes, deep blue like Cliff's, lit up with unbelieving joy. His freckled face shone. "Oh, can I?" he said. "Can I? Oh, gee!" He was back in the vestibule in a flash.

"You didn't have to do that," Cliff said. "You don't have to spoil the pageant. He doesn't need to have his own way."

Jeanie said gently, "This time, I think he does." She added, "It won't spoil the pageant. We don't *know* there were only three Wise Men. Tradition says so, but didn't someone write a story about the fourth Wise Man? Anyway, who knows there weren't four? Tonight there will be."

Cliff's voice was warm. "You're quite a girl," he said. "Why haven't I seen you around?"

To her great annoyance, Jeanie felt herself blushing again. "We've only been in town a few weeks," she said. "Dad was transferred by his company. We don't know anybody here." She wondered miserably why she couldn't think of something bright and interesting to say.

Tommy loped down the aisle, the bathrobe enveloping his small figure. "I'm ready," he said breathlessly.

Jeanie smoothed the robe. She took her blue scarf and draped it around his head. "This will do for now," she said. She reached for a vase of flowers on the altar rail. "You can use this for a gift. I'll bring something more appropriate for you to carry tonight. Now go join the other three, and we'll go through the scene again. Tell the boys to sing, 'We Four Kings of Orient Are'."

"*Thank* you," he said. "Oh, thank you!" He scampered off to join the others.

"You're good with kids," Cliff said, and his eyes held admiration. "Really good. I don't know whether you'd be interested or not, but I'm going to be working with the park department here in Center City this summer—recreation, play, things like that. I'll be needing an assistant. I think you'd be great."

"I'd love it," Jeanie said. "It would be wonderful." And

it would. She would be a real part of Center City. And she would be working with Cliff. Her heart gave a leap of happiness. She forced her attention back to the stage.

The children were all grouped around the manger. Susan Mitchell was looking lovingly at the cradle, a radiant smile on her face which the missing tooth didn't seem to mar. The Heavenly Host were quiet, too.

The four Wise Men knelt in front of the manger, reverently placing their gold, and frankincense, and myrrh, and a little bunch of wilted flowers, at the foot of the cradle. The organist began the music for the last hymn, and the soft childish voices chimed in. "Silent night, holy night. All is calm, all is bright." Tommy's clear voice rang out above the others.

Tears pricked at Jeanie's eyes. Christmas was wonderful! Always. Wherever you were. She felt a sudden rush of love for them all. Susan and Tommy, and the fat littlest angel with his halo tilted over one eye.

Cliff smiled down at her. "Merry Christmas, Jeanie," he said.

She smiled back. "Merry Christmas, Cliff."

Then the rehearsal was over, the quiet shattered into the confusion of taking off costumes and struggling into coats and hats.

Cliff managed to get Jeanie alone for a minute. "I'll come back tonight and help," he said. "That is, if you can use me."

"Oh, I can," she said. "You've been great!"

"Look," he said, "there's a dance at the Club on Wednesday night. A Christmas dance. I didn't think I'd go, but all of a sudden I'd like to. I'd like to a lot, if you'll go with me."

A vision of the red taffeta dress floated in front of Jeanie's eyes. Miracles did happen at Christmas! Even very small ones, like hers—and Tommy's. "I'd love to go," she said.

Tommy tugged at Cliff's sleeve, his blue eyes bright with

happiness. "Isn't she wunnerful, Cliff? Isn't she just wunnerful?"

Cliff rumpled the small boy's hair. "You know what, Jeanie? I think he *is* a wise man. A very wise man."

Jeanie laughed, and Cliff laughed. And Tommy laughed too, even though he didn't know why they were laughing.

"Merry Christmas, everybody," he said.

From Six to Midnight

J. P. FOLLINSBEE

WELL, it isn't as though you absolutely *had* to go,"
Margy said, the telephone connection lending
a note of complaint to her tone. "After all, it's
volunteer work. And they can't expect us to give up
everything!"

Cath sighed, and switched the receiver to her other ear.
"You make it sound almost as though I were doing something wrong."

"Well, you are—sort of." Margy's voice bounced back,
aggrieved. "After all, if *you* give up the High Harvest Hop
to go mousing around the hospital, they'll expect *all* of us
to be at their beck and call." She paused, then added
hastily, "Oh, I don't mean that, exactly. Everybody knows
how important it is to help out at the hospital. But to turn
down a date like *this!*"

"I know. Don't think I'm deliriously happy about it,"
Cath defended herself. "It's only—well, this past month

hardly anyone has kept our schedule. And I just can't let them down—not after I said I'd come."

"Well, of course," Margy's voice stiffened. "You may happen to enjoy being a nurse's aide. But I know if I'd had a chance to make a fourth for the dance with Bob Allen, no gloomy old hospital would have held me back. Honestly, Cath, a new boy in school just a few weeks, and he hasn't even spoken to a girl, hardly. And then he asks Tommy to arrange a foursome. My gosh, anyone else would have given a leg for a chance like that. If you're not careful, people will think you're a regular dope, Cath."

The words hurt, and Cath bit her lower lip. Still, there was no use flaring up at Margy. A date with Bob Allen would have been a triumph. She could have called and said she couldn't make it—just this once. Miss Morrow, the head nurse, was always patient and understanding, no matter how feeble the excuses some of the girls offered.

"O.K., so I'm a dope," she sighed. "Margy, I've got to get ready—it's almost six."

"Look," Margy said, "you could even go, and then get a headache. The dance won't really start until ten. And Bob will be there—stag. He told Tommy he'd have his father's car. Just think," Margy's voice rose excitedly, "you could sweep in—a heroine. Nurse Pearson, fresh from her duties on the wards!"

It was a ridiculous suggestion, but Cath felt a tingle of excitement.

"I hadn't thought of going later," she said slowly. "I suppose if it was a quiet night, and there wasn't too much to do . . ."

"Of course!" Margy's voice leaped into the pause. "That's it! You could be home by eight-thirty, changed by nine. Tommy and I could pick you up. Oh, Cath, do it! This is your big chance to make Bob Allen yours, exclusively!"

"Well . . ." Cath hesitated. "Maybe. But I'll probably

get tied up. Please don't say anything to Bob." She had to hang up! Otherwise, in a moment she might commit herself and be sorry afterward. "Look, Margy, I've got to go now. I'll be late. 'Bye."

She cradled the receiver hastily. A *dope*. The gang must have been talking. Oh, just after-school Coke gossip, probably. But still . . .

She started down the hall to the kitchen. It would be so simple to say she had a headache. Miss Morrow would understand. On the other hand, she had helped organize the High Aide Auxiliary, and she, of all people, couldn't afford to let it down. Lynwood Hospital needed help so desperately. The least she could do was to try to keep the Auxiliary from dwindling away completely.

This was silly, of course. If the others didn't want to go, that was their privilege. What had Miss Morrow said when they first approached her? *Any help you can give will be deeply appreciated.* Miss Morrow, with years of experience in working with volunteer groups, hadn't expected too much. Perhaps Margy was right. It was fine to do things if you enjoyed them. But when they became a grind, then maybe it was asking too much. . . .

She poked her head in the kitchen doorway. Her mother was busy at the stove.

"Hi, chef," Cath called. "I'm on my way."

Her mother glanced up anxiously. "So soon, Cath? Why don't you wait until your father comes home, and let him drive you? It's a perfectly dreadful night out."

"I'll run for the bus," Cath smiled. "It'll have me there in a jiff."

"All right." Her mother looked at her searchingly. "Not sorry now—about missing the dance, Cath?"

"Sure—but I'll live." She tried for a light tone. "Margy says I'm turning into a dope."

"Oh. Is that terribly bad?"

"Well, it isn't exactly high praise." She hesitated.

"Mom, if you do happen to have a minute after dinner, would you mind taking a look at my white formal? See if there are any wrinkles? I thought, maybe—well, if it happens to be one of those quiet nights at the hospital, Miss Morrow could perhaps let me slip off early." *It wasn't exactly a lie. She wouldn't confront Miss Morrow with an old chestnut like a headache. She would tell her honestly. . . .*

"Of course, dear. But, *who* . . . ?"

"Margy says Bob Allen is going stag," Cath explained quickly. "She and Tommy would pick me up, you see. Oh, it probably won't come to anything. But I thought . . . well, I don't know. I'm late, Mom. I'll have to rush."

The icy October rain flooded in sheets against the windows of the bus, turning the streets into a watery, eerie glow of lights. It was getting very cold. Peering through the glass, Cath watched the library glide past. Four more blocks.

She shivered. It seemed so unfair. You tried to do what you thought was right. But it wasn't as if Three H was just *any* dance. If only Miss Morrow would say, "I don't think we need you tonight, Pearson." But that would be asking for a miracle.

And Margy was right. Bob Allen probably wouldn't ask her again. It was crazy, but even that afternoon last week when he and Tommy had sauntered into the soda bar so casually, she had felt herself go a little weak.

"Hi, there!" Tommy had called out, and had come galloping over to where she and Margy were sitting. "May we sit?"

"This is Bob Allen, as you well know," Tommy said. "We just put him on the team. Boy, you should see him hit that basket! Margy and Cath, Bob. I warn you, they're inseparable!"

"How do you like Lynnwood, Bob?" Cath asked. "I'm afraid it must seem tame—after Chicago."

"No." He shook his head. "I like it better. I was glad when Dad's company transferred him here. I guess we're what you'd call small-town folks." He stopped, suddenly embarrassed.

"Well," Tommy put in, with the finesse of a meat chopper, "we're short on night life—unless you like dancing, that is. Three H next Friday."

A deep flush rose over Bob's face, and Cath wished the floor would swallow her up.

"I know," Bob rallied. "Tommy says you and he are going." He glanced toward Margy. Then he looked at Cath and the crimson flowed back. "I know it's kind of short notice. But I was asking Tommy, here, and—well, I was wondering if you would care—if we could make it a foursome?"

It was an invitation she hadn't dared dream about. Most of the boys, with the advantage of years of growing up together, asked for a date as though they were tossing you a bone. But somehow she had known that Bob wasn't the confident type who played the field, and he would have withered with embarrassment if he had even suspected how much the girls had discussed him.

And she had turned him down! As Margy would say, she had muffed her big chance . . . and for what? A dreary night in the wards.

The locker room in the Nurses' Quarters was deserted. It was certainly an awful night for the dance. Yet it would be fun to swirl around the gym while the storm raged outside. You would feel cut off from the world, like storm-bound passengers at sea. . . .

She shook the thought from her mind, and changed quickly. Usually she enjoyed putting on her uniform, but tonight the stiff cloth felt harsh—almost unpleasant to touch. She caught her brown hair into a net and stood back. She had become someone else. It was almost as though changing clothes changed your identity and made you a part of the great, impersonal, and yet very human hospital around you. You became a cog, an anonymous worker—a grind.

She brushed her hand against her forehead. It did feel a little warm. She glanced at her watch. Just five minutes to six! If she stayed until eight—her pulse quickened. *Just this once surely Miss Morrow would understand!*

Miss Morrow, at the desk in the Chart Room on Women's Surgery, looked up as Cath came in.

"I'm glad you could make it, Pearson," she said. "Colson and Andrews are out with some sort of virus."

Cath's heart sank. She might have known! Miracles certainly *didn't* happen—not at Lynnwood, anyway.

"I'm sorry," she said. *Probably right this moment her mother was laying out her formal. And Margy was calling Tommy to come late.*

Miss Morrow went on, "I'm afraid I'm going to have to ask you to help in both Surgery and Children's Ward tonight. You might start in there, if you like. Take down the supper trays, and get the scamps settled for the night." She glanced at her watch. "Visitors in ten minutes. Chase them all out by seven."

"Yes, Miss Morrow." It was just like the Army. Orders, orders, orders. Choking back her disappointment, she tried to make her mind grasp the problems ahead. Miss Morrow's cryptic remarks implied a thousand little duties. Settling the Children's Ward was always like soothing bedlam. And tonight, of all nights!

Her heels clicked angrily as she walked down the hushed, antiseptic-odored hallway. A loudspeaker called for Doctor Peterson, and she frowned at it. At least *that* would stop after nine o'clock.

Suddenly, for no reason at all, she felt like crying. She had hoped—almost needed, in fact—one word of gratitude from Miss Morrow. One word of encouragement. The nurse could so easily have said it was wonderful of her to come in such horrible weather. But, instead, a cool, crisp, "Glad you could make it, Pearson."

No wonder Margy thought she was a fool! Instead of walking down this cold, smelly hall, she could be racing from a scented bath to her frothy white gown. Instead of walking into a ward full of petulant, attention-demanding kids, she could be floating down the stairs to Bob.

She hesitated. Surely sometimes you were entitled to think of yourself. Miss Morrow obviously didn't appreciate her coming. So, she would stay until eight o'clock. On the dot. Then she would walk into Miss Morrow's office. Maybe a headache wasn't very original, but after all— And even with Colson and Andrews off, the hospital would manage somehow. It always had in the past.

The children's crying coincided exactly with the departure of the last visitors. Cath's arms ached from carrying supper trays, remaking beds under squirming young bodies, administering bed baths, changing dressings and diapers, and picking up the debris of toys and more toys. But she didn't feel tired. Time seemed to be floating by. *In exactly an hour she would be racing home. She could probably have a hot bath, and be ready by nine. . . .*

It was time for the rounds of bedtime stories, cajoling, and mild threats that would eventually result in peace and quiet. She felt herself looking forward to it with a mixture of guilt and exhilaration. With the children settled, the worst would be over.

"You take on the older ones," Evans said, passing with a stack of linens. Almost without thinking, Cath passed the back of her hand to her forehead and smiled wanly. Evans stopped. "What's the matter? Headache?"

Cath nodded. "It's nothing," she said. "I'll be all right."

"Well, I'll do the babies and fix some tea afterwards. Tea is always good." Evans smiled with motherly concern, and went on.

Cath looked after her, her heart pounding. *It was so easy! Really, no one need suspect at all.* . . .

She turned into a semi-private room where young Dicky Anderson—in traction with a broken femur—was loudly proclaiming his misery.

She smiled down at the fretful youngster. "What's the matter, Dicky?"

"I'm scared," he said, his voice tiny and tearful. "Last night I had a bad dream and nobody came. I was scared *awful!* A big thing was climbing on the ropes and nobody came!"

"Well, if he comes back tonight, you just call and I . . ." She stopped. "Miss Evans will come, I know, and chase him away. Now try to go to sleep. I'll leave the night light on, see?" She flicked the main switch, leaving the room in a soft glow. "Now, you don't see any big old things, do you?"

"Where are *you* going?" he demanded. "Why won't you come and chase him away?"

She sighed. "Well, I might be somewhere else, don't you see? I might not hear you."

He gazed at her doubtfully. "I wish you wouldn't go away," he whispered. "You're nice. Please don't go away."

She looked down at his pale face. If he had a bad dream tonight, no one would "hear" either. Evans, alone on the ward, would be far too busy to do more than glance in.

She pushed back an imaginary lock of hair, and sat again on the bed. "Dicky"—she began, and stopped. It was no use. All the time she and Bob were dancing, she would be wondering, and feeling guilty. It was fine to do things if you enjoyed them. But she wouldn't be able to enjoy the dance. Not now.

It happened just after ten o'clock. Dimly, her mind registered the wail of a siren fading down the drive. She speculated briefly and dismissed it. Probably nothing important.

Then the ghostly voice of the public address system stopped her. It was never used after nine o'clock!

"Nurses," Miss Morrow's voice said coolly. "All but essential duty nurses report to my office at once." A chill swept down Cath's arms.

The voice repeated the message and squeaked into silence. Cath's feet raced. Unceremoniously, she slipped the hot water bag under Mrs. Forest's bedclothes and dashed into the hall.

The utter silence of a moment ago had whispered into footsteps, hurrying and urgent. A second ambulance wailed down the drive. All around her, Cath could feel the pulse of the hospital quickening. She broke into a run.

Miss Morrow's voice was controlled.

"We have a serious emergency," she said. "A bus accident on Crescent Drive. We'll need fifteen beds. Only two are presently available in Emergency, one in Maternity."

Cath's breath caught. With a shock she realized that, even including herself, there were only five nurses present. She had forgotten how small the hospital was, how desperately cramped for space and help. Thank heavens, she thought, for Dicky's bad dream!

"Allen and Greenwood stand by in receiving. Paulson, Emergency. Set up three cots, four if you can cram them in. Stein, Men's Surgery. Move your ambulatories into chairs for now, we'll find beds later." Miss Morrow's pencil hesitated as she checked down her list. Then she looked up. "Pearson, can you manage three beds in Women's Surgery, and a cot in Children's?"

"Yes," Cath answered. *There were no beds, but still you could make no other reply.* You couldn't even hesitate. It was not a question, it was a command.

"Good. Apparently only four cases are serious. Five may be discharged after treatment, but we can't afford to count on it. Avoid disturbing the other patients as much as possible. That's all."

Cath turned with the others and hurried from the office. It was incredible! She was not a nurse, and yet suddenly she must act as one. For the first time, she would have to make decisions, she would have to find beds where there were no beds. For a panicky moment she almost turned back. Miss Morrow would have to send someone else—someone who *knew* what to do.

But even as she hesitated, the cold, implacable truth became a reality. *There was no one else!* Colson and Andrews were sick, leaving an irreparable gap—a gap she had almost widened. Miss Morrow had charged her to fill it—somehow.

Suddenly, she was no longer frightened. There had to be a way.

She pushed open the ward doors. Miraculously, Jimmy, one of the orderlies, was waiting. In her relief, the solution came, automatically, out of nowhere.

"Jimmy," she said, "can you move Mrs. Sanders' bed in with Mrs. Beck in Private A? I'll make up the sun porch for Mrs. Forest and Mrs. Connors. That way we'll keep the three emergencies together in the semi-private if you can find a spare bed or cot. There's a fold-up in the ward closet."

He nodded and disappeared.

Cath folded back the covers on the bed as Jimmy and Smitty maneuvered the stretcher through the door and brought it alongside. The patient—a young woman now almost unrecognizably bandaged—was still deep in an anesthetic sleep.

Cath cradled the patient's head as the orderlies lifted the girl gently into bed. Only a part of her still, white face was visible, and Cath found herself wondering if there would be scars.

"Well, that's the last," Jimmy whispered in relief. "Over two hours on the table." Then, almost as though he heard Cath's thought, he added, "She's lucky, though. Face hardly touched. She must have ducked as they went over."

Cath nodded. "How are the others?" She kept her voice low as she adjusted the cool blankets.

"All O.K., apparently." Jimmy wheeled the stretcher to the door. "It beats me. Somebody should have been killed."

Cath began a last check of the ward. The other two emergencies—neither seriously hurt—had long since drifted into a deep, drugged sleep.

She smiled, and clicked off the glowing wall lamp. In the dim, pinkish glow of the night light, the ward at last seemed utterly at peace.

In the corridor, she glanced at her watch, checking the time for her report. *Five minutes to one!*

Where had the hours gone? She had better call home at once. But first, she'd check with Miss Morrow.

She hurried. The last three hours had simply vanished in a nightmare of preparing beds, checking identifications, notifying next-of-kin, hovering on call for plasma, dressings —a million little things, all carried out in a tense, controlled silence. Few of the other patients had even awakened. In the Children's Ward, only Dicky's voice had called out— from a bad dream.

Suddenly, the thought came. *The dance would be over! And she hadn't even thought of it—not once, after expecting to live with it every moment through the endless hours from six to midnight.*

She smiled, and let the ache of weariness take over her arms and shoulders. It was wonderful to be so tired, so wonderfully, happily tired.

Miss Morrow and Evans were working on a mass of papers in Miss Morrow's office. "Oh, Pearson," Miss Morrow looked up, "how are your patients?"

Her patients! She hadn't thought of it in that way. But— tonight, at least—it had been true.

"Sleeping quietly," she reported. "They just brought the abrasion case down. She's going to be all right, Jimmy says."

"Good." Miss Morrow smiled. "I was just about to send

for you. Your father called about fifteen minutes ago. He's probably in the waiting room now."

"I'll go right down." Cath hesitated. "If you like, I could come again tomorrow," she offered. "I thought with Colson and Andrews off, and . . ."

"It would be wonderful if you could." Miss Morrow's eyes flickered almost imperceptibly. How exhausted she must be! "And Pearson, I—can't thank you enough for tonight and all the other nights. So I won't try. It's been a good job, that's all."

A *good job!* Cath walked proudly down the corridor. Those three simple words, from Miss Morrow, meant more than volumes of praise.

Her eyes shining, she started down the stairs. *Thank heaven, she hadn't pleaded a headache.* She decided to cut through the waiting room and tell her father she would meet him at the car.

Then, at the door, she stopped. The room was filled with people. Of course! Relatives. She had forgotten how an accident reached out and touched so many lives.

Her father was standing a little apart, near the door. She raised her hand to catch his eye, and in the same instant she saw Bob.

She retreated quickly and slipped into the information booth adjoining the waiting room.

Cath's finger ran down the registry of patients. The emergencies were hastily added at the end. And there it was. *Robert Allen.* Bob's father.

"Mildred," she whispered, "could you get me Men's Surgery, please?"

"Sure," Mildred nodded. "Take it on the house phone." A moment later, she knew. He had come in with the others. A mild concussion. Should be discharged in a day or two.

She hesitated. Perhaps it would be better just to slip away. But that would be adolescent. She returned to the waiting room.

"Hello, Dad." She smiled as he came to her. "I'll meet

you at the car in three minutes. Where are you parked?"

"Down at the west end of the drive. We were getting worried."

"I'll be right there." She nodded toward Bob. "I just want to speak to Bob a minute. His father was in the accident—nothing serious, fortunately."

Her pulse quickened as she made her way through the crowd toward him.

"Hello, Bob," she said quietly.

He looked up and sprang to his feet.

"Cath!" he said. "I was so wrapped up I didn't recognize you."

"I was sorry to learn about your father, Bob. I just found out a moment ago. He was in another wing."

"I got the news at the dance." He looked down. "I can't help blaming myself," he said. "If I hadn't taken the car tonight, it would never have happened."

"But that's foolish!" She sounded exactly like Miss Morrow, she thought, and went on in a gentler tone. "He might have taken a bus ten minutes earlier or ten minutes later, too, you know."

Bob nodded. "I hadn't thought of it in quite that way," he said slowly. He looked up and smiled briefly. "I thought of your being here tonight. It seemed strange. After the dance, and all—and then Dad. . . ."

"I know." She understood so well how he felt, but she couldn't say it. "Why don't you go home, Bob? I'm afraid they won't let you see your father tonight. But I'm sure he's going to be all right."

"I suppose I should." He hesitated, awkwardly. "I don't suppose I could take you home?"

"Thanks, Bob—but Dad's waiting." Margy would have called that muffing your big chance. But there was time, now. They didn't have to speak of it, or say anything more.

"Of course." His eyes caught hers. "Tomorrow, then? Could I call you?"

She smiled. "Tomorrow will be fine."

The Brave
in Heart

SYLVIE SCHUMAN

A CHILL gray light fell through the rimed corridor windows, heightening an odd premonition that pressed in her.

She took the stairs to the *Tattler* office slowly, thankful for once that there were no elevators at Plainview High. How would she ever live through this meeting? Grant and the gang there at once.

She stopped in the middle of the stairway. She wouldn't attend. She'd plead a headache. But her feet started again of their own volition. It was an important meeting. Things were going to pop. They didn't like Miss Sands. A new teacher—one starting in the middle of the term at that—shouldn't make demands, have different ideas. It was Sands who'd suggested Grant join the *Tattler*. She'd noticed his poems in the school magazine and read his themes aloud in class. Yes, Grant was her pet. That was another thing the gang couldn't forgive. . . . Her heart thudded as she pushed open the glass door on which was an inked sign, *Tattler*, and underneath in smaller letters, *Infirmary*.

Peggy's eyes scanned the room and caught the faded blue sweater she was looking for—the crooked bow-tie. She took the chair Anne had saved for her, observing that Anne was even paler than usual, that the air was electric with tension. The editor-in-chief's chair was empty.

Anne whispered, "Arthur's late on purpose, of course."

Miss Sands was removing her turban, and her Mexican earrings shook. The girls thought her dowdy. Those beige dresses and her short ash-blond hair! A draught flew in, and the door closed behind Arthur Bates. Even now, two years after her silly sophomore crush on him, Peggy was still impressed.

"Hello, hello," he said briskly. His eyes slid past Miss Sands and ignored Grant. "Are we ready?" He looked around the room with an air of belonging and ease.

Miss Sands smiled, but there was no answering welcome. "I think you all know Grant Dyke. He writes so well, I thought *Tattler* could use him."

"Uh, Miss Sands," Arthur broke in, "not that I have anything against Dyke, but . . ." his hand gestured around the room, "we're so crowded here, we can't move. This is really the infirmary, as you know—and that first aid cabinet takes a whole wall. We only managed by removing the cot, so I don't see how we can take on anyone."

Peggy's words came out with a little rush. "We can always squeeze in one more person, Arthur."

His look was icy, but Miss Sands took her up. "Of course, we can. I thought Grant could do book reviews for us. His reports are always so vivid and interesting."

That's how it had started—with a book report, *Look Homeward, Angel*. It was wonderful how Grant had caught perfectly the inspired mood Peggy had felt reading Thomas Wolfe. She remembered Arthur Bates attacking the report. Old Lady Thompson, their former teacher, had always favored Arthur. There had been an added mutiny among Arthur's followers that had brought red patches to Miss Sands' cheeks.

At the end of the class, Peggy had found herself at Grant's side. "Your report was wonderful," she said. They walked home together, Peggy only half-conscious of the stares that followed them. They made a date for Saturday.

She was jerked back to the meeting by the sound of raised voices. "I still insist the kids don't give a hoot about book reviews," Arthur was saying.

Anne disagreed. "I'm all for a book column, and I think Grant would do a wonderful job." Peggy seconded Anne, and it was settled that Grant would do the column.

But Miss Sands' next words started a rivulet of fear in Peggy. "I've been studying *Tattler*," she said. "We have too many gossip columns. We'll have to drop one to make room for the books."

"The kids like gossip," Peggy's voice was edged with resentment. "They eat it up. They only buy *Tattler* for the personal items."

But Miss Sands went on. "I want you to look closely at this paper." She unfolded the *Merrimac Mouthpiece*. "It won the National Scholastic Award last year for the best school newspaper. Notice—two columns of gossip on the back page. On the front, school problems, an editorial, even community affairs."

Peggy hardened herself against the speech. . . . Her column—her one small claim to distinction—no one must take that away. . . .

With panic, she saw Miss Sands turning to her. "Now, Peggy, *you* write so well, it's a shame to waste you on gossip."

"I don't think it's a waste," she said fiercely. "And why pick on me? Rhoda has a column, too—and so have Arthur and Tim—"

"Mine is the lead column," Rhoda blazed. "Yours is only about fashion. We could do without that."

Miss Sands never even looked at Rhoda. It was as though she were trying to convey a message to Peggy. "I know that later you'll find something you really want to write about," she said.

Peggy bit her lips, forcing back tears. She hid her burning face, pretending to search for a handkerchief in her purse. Why had she voted for the book column?

"I'm not going to force you," Miss Sands was saying. "As citizens you're free. I'm only hoping that you'll use your freedom. This is your world, and you should have a say in it."

Through her misery, Peggy could see that the air had taken on a new note of tension. She had missed something. Arthur was on the point of bursting. "I think it's none of our business," he bit out.

"But this is your school," Miss Sands went on gravely. "You're the ones who are crowded here. You told me so yourself. Conditions are bad. The vote to enlarge Plainview High School which comes up in a few weeks concerns you more than your parents. I definitely think *Tattler* should take a stand."

"I agree," Grant put in. "I certainly think we could devote an editorial to it. *Tattler* editorials are always about football—or the weather."

Beside Peggy, Anne was in the thick of it. It was bad for Anne to get excited. Delicate, pale Anne was kept out of things by her health. "I think it would be wonderful to have a fighting newspaper. We could even get the kids in on it. We could have a letters column where they say what they think. I'd run it. I'd do the work at home."

So Anne was with Miss Sands, too. Anne and Grant. She looked up, and her glance collided with his. She turned away.

"What do *you* think, Peg?" Arthur was asking suddenly.

"You're the only one we haven't heard from. Surely you don't support our taking a stand on such an issue."

Before Peggy could say no, Anne jumped in. "That's not fair, putting the question to her that way."

Peggy was conscious of everyone's watching her intently. She glanced away from the plea in Miss Sands' eyes and from the command in Arthur's. She dared not look at Grant. "I don't know. I haven't made up my mind yet."

Miss Sands shut her briefcase. "We'll have to hold the vote till next week." She looked keenly at Peggy. "The deciding vote is yours . . ."

She must have been lying in bed, staring at the ceiling for hours. It had stopped sleeting, and a dull purplish light arrowed into her bedroom. Beside her lay the blue bound notebook in which she jotted odd thoughts, little word pictures of people who impressed her. It was her secret book—and only Anne had ever read it. Tonight she had added some bitter phrases to the profile of Miss Sands. The piece on Grant was a crumpled ball in the wastebasket. . . . Distantly she heard her brother scampering to open the front door, and a moment later Anne's smile flew at her from the doorway. "Moping—or dreaming?"

She sat up. "I hate everything and especially Miss Sands."

Anne's fragile features sobered. "Your friends Arthur and Rhoda sold you out, didn't they?"

"It was Miss Sands' fault."

Anne's mouth was skeptical. "You're going to vote for the editorial?" she demanded.

Peggy's chin went stubborn. "I told you I don't know yet."

"But you've complained about school conditions a million times. You . . ." Anne stopped herself. "You're doing it for spite—and—you'd disappoint Grant terribly."

Peggy turned scarlet. "Does that matter? I don't ever want to see him again."

Anne's voice softened. "I wish Grant Dyke liked me. Oh, don't act so surprised. And don't pity me. I'm satisfied with things the way they are. If only you'd get off the fence. . . ."

"Really, Anne, I don't want to talk about it." She broke off to pop her head out the door. The phone had been ringing insistently and her brother was calling upstairs. When she turned back, her face was agitated. "It's Grant —he's coming over . . ."

Anne rose quickly. "I'll slip out." She added, "Peggy, try to live on your best side some time."

She felt unanchored with Anne gone. She washed and changed into a cheerful plaid, her heart thumping, her mind trying to decipher Anne's last words.

When she opened the door to Grant, her hand in his was cold.

"I suppose you're sore at me," he said. "I didn't expect my coming on *Tattler* would end up with your losing out. I guess I spell trouble for you."

She glanced quickly at him. What did he mean? "It was Sands' fault."

"You're being foolish!"

"Am I?"

"She picked on you because she thinks you've got stuff, don't you see? Rhoda's a dumb Dora—she can tell that at a glance. She wanted you to help her put life into the paper —eliminate some of that junk in it."

"So she started by eliminating me. What am I supposed to do—set a good example for the others by being a willing sacrifice?"

Grant put his hand on her arm. "Let's walk down to the Tambor for some waffles. I want to talk to you about this."

At the Tambor Grant said calmly, "In a way, I'm glad you lost that column."

She stared and made a motion to rise. "Don't you even want to know why?" She sat down again. "Because you've got the makings of a real person in you," Grant went on, "but you keep running away with Arthur and Rhoda and that ilk. Just because they can't see Miss Sands—won't give her a chance—you're jumping on the bandwagon with them. Why, she's the best thing that ever hit Plainview High. She's got guts—she—"

Peggy injected tartly, "And she likes you. Let's not forget that."

"That doesn't sound like you. It sounds like the others. A pack of sheep—all thinking, talking, dressing the same way. Afraid of anything different."

"You have no right to—you—"

He smiled. "Go ahead—use all the labels. You think I don't know them? Apple-polisher, bookworm, wallflower, character, drip. . . . Paper bullets—they've shot me with them, but I don't fall down. I happen not to be like the gang. Dancing and baseball are not sacred to me."

The room seemed to be pitching around her. "I never said those things . . ."

"But you've felt them." That smile played around his lips again.

She began to protest. "I don't know how we got started on all this. What's it got to do with my column—and Miss Sands?"

He reached over suddenly and took her hand. "It goes deeper than you think. I'm trying to show you that Miss Sands is a friend."

She jerked her hand from his grasp. "Maybe she's *your* friend . . ."

Something ignited in his eyes. "You're a coward, Peggy Smith. Go ahead—play it safe, and on Friday vote against the editorial."

The words came from her coldly. "I think you've said enough, Grant Dyke." She grabbed her coat. "I'll thank you never to speak to me again." She hurried out blindly, aware of the waiter staring after her.

She walked quickly, hands in her pockets, anger foaming in her. She felt shaken and lost in the windy street. Presently she found herself heading toward Rhoda's.

The blue college banner hung over a saggy studio couch in Rhoda's basement rumpus room. A couple were drinking sodas, and Rhoda and Arthur were dancing to the blare of a radio. In the corner one girl was showing another some new dance steps. The familiar scene wrapped around Peggy cosily, blanking out the memory of Grant.

"Well—well. . . ." Arthur danced Rhoda over. "How come you're not holdings hands with Dyke—thrilling to Shakespeare?"

Rhoda turned wide eyes to Arthur. "Maybe he's going to do her book reports for her."

Peggy said, "I'm sorry I ever voted for the column. I'm finished with Dyke."

"He's a drip. Why waste breath on him? We'll get him off *Tattler*—Sands, too."

"What do you mean?" she shivered a little.

He turned to Rhoda with an expression Peggy couldn't read and said, "How about getting us some sodas?" Then he held out an arm to Peggy. "Dance?"

It was a slow number, and she was suddenly aware of his holding her closer than usual. "You got me very sore this afternoon, Peg," he said close to her ear. "I mean—siding with that guy. Just when I was going to ask you to the prom, too."

She stared. "Me? But. . . ." Her eyes flew to Rhoda.

"Rhoda's going with Tim. We've kind of—cooled, shall we say?"

It didn't seem possible that Arthur Bates would be looking at her this way, coaxing her cheek against his. "I've got plans for us, Peg. Funny, it hit me when I saw you with Dyke. I realized I was jealous." He put a finger under her chin and lifted her face to his. "You *are* finished with him —for good?"

His eyes held her. "For good."

The days went feverishly for Peggy. Time was suddenly chockful of Arthur. They danced, went to the movies, lingered over hot chocolates and fudge sundaes. She reveled in it. Anything to blot out Grant Dyke.

Thursday Anne phoned. "I see you caught the gold ring on the merry-go-round. . . . I've missed you. . . ."

Peggy apologized. "It'll slow down. It's the first fine careless rapture."

"Is it?" Anne's voice held an odd emphasis. "Peggy—maybe it's not right asking about this, but tomorrow's the vote."

"I've made up my mind. I'm voting against it." The phone seemed to go dead. "Anne . . . hello . . . ?"

Anne's voice came distantly. "I'm here, Peggy. I feel bad about this. It goes deeper than you think."

Grant's exact words. "My mother's calling," she fibbed. "See you tomorrow."

At the meeting Arthur's eyes gleamed triumphantly; seemed to say, "We'll fix Sands today, won't we?"

Peggy looked through Grant as though he were glass. Anne had dark rings under her eyes, and her skin had a sickly pallor. She scanned Peggy's face hopefully, then her eyes darkened.

Miss Sands started abruptly. "Well, Peggy, made up your mind?"

You could hear a pin drop. She stared straight ahead. "I'm voting a . . ." And suddenly something beside her was sliding. There was a thudding sound, a clatter of books. The room erupted into action. "Get the smelling salts," someone called. Peggy's hand trembled, scrambling among the jammed bottles in the cabinet. Miss Sands was cradling Anne's head. "Pick her up—somebody!" Peggy cried. "Oh, there's no salts. I'll have to go for water. . . ." Anne looked pitiful on the oak floor. Peggy's voice rose. "Must she lie there?"

Grant turned grimly to her. "What do you want us to do? There's no cot here, remember? There's no nurse—we've disgraceful conditions in this school, or has that escaped you?"

"Get water," Miss Sands said sharply and Peggy fled down the corridor.

Four flights down to the only drinking fountain. A person could die in that time. Her hand shook as she filled the paper cup. She had to go up slowly to keep it from spilling. Poor Anne—the picture of her on the floor came back painfully. Why weren't there supplies in that big clumsy cabinet? Something should be done about such conditions. But that was what Miss Sands had said all along.

"I haven't even considered the principle involved," Peggy thought. "All I've been thinking about is my pride."

Anne's eyelids fluttered open as Peggy put the water to her lips. "I got too excited," she murmured. "I'm all right now." They helped her to a chair. "Really, I'm all right. Go ahead with the vote. Or is it all over . . . ?"

Peggy's voice was large and firm. "I vote for *Tattler* to take a stand on the school enlargement issue."

Looking back on it, it didn't seem possible to Peggy that just those few words could cause so much to happen. But like a tiny atomic explosion, they created a chain reaction. The detonations were somehow hazy in her mind now, blending into one big ache. . . . The very thought of Arthur made her feel soiled. He'd banged his fist on the desk. "If this editorial appears, I'm resigning."

There had been a grumbling commotion. Even Tim, who had been on Arthur's side, didn't like sore losers. She would never forget Arthur's stiffness as he walked out and how awful she'd felt that she'd had to let him down. But the next moment Rhoda had followed him out.

"I guess we'll both lose our prom dates if we don't go after them," Peggy said to Tim.

He looked blank. "I had no prom date with Rhoda. She's

going with Arthur. She told me so herself—just this morning." Suddenly his eyes narrowed. "Say—was that what they
were trying to pull on you so you'd vote. . . ." She'd fled
from the pity in his eyes. . . .

At the next meeting she broke her silence toward Grant.
He had read his editorial aloud, his voice shaking a little.
"As the vocal body of Plainview High, we feel we must take
up the cudgels for our fellow students. This is our world.
We must fight to improve it." He stood half in light, and
there were ridges of shadow on his face, giving it a Lin-
colnesque quality.

There was spontaneous applause when Grant finished.
She stayed when the others left. "Your editorial was wonderful." It was almost as though it were the first time she'd
spoken to him.

He busied himself with his manuscript. "Isn't this where
I came in . . . ?"

"Grant." He looked at her, his eyes remote. "You were
right. I was a coward."

She saw something like hope spring into his face, but
he said, "I wish I could trust you, Peg. . . ." Tears welled
to her eyes, and she started out, hoping he would call her
back. But he didn't.

The weeks ticked off in memories. Nothing seemed to
reach her. Not even the success of the new *Tattler*. Like a
bystander, she observed the commotion the editorial stirred
up. Even when she stood in the midst of the rally which
the editorial had encouraged, only one part of her was alive.
The other was always looking for Grant.

Perversely it was when the real triumph came that Peggy
felt she could go on no more. Grant got the news first and
rushed to *Tattler* with it. "We've won. I just got it from the
Star. The enlargement vote went through last night—over-
whelmingly." Miss Sands wrung Grant's hand, and her
face glowed. Anne cried, "Yippee," and hugged Peggy. Tim
pumped Grant's hand. "It was your editorial that did it."

They were so busy congratulating each other, they didn't see the principal enter. He cleared his throat. "Not that I want you to stop rejoicing," he said. "But I think you should read this."

He handed Miss Sands an envelope. Her eyes scanned the letter quickly, and when she looked up, Peggy saw tears.

Miss Sands handed the letter back to Mr. Macy.

"Won't you read it aloud at assembly hall today?" he asked. "Everyone should hear it. Er, Miss Sands, I'd like to speak to you alone in my office."

They were in a panic of conjecture until assembly. And then Mr. Macy was addressing them. "I want to read a letter which arrived at my desk this morning." He adjusted his horn rims. "This is to notify you that the *Tattler* is the winner of the annual scholastic award for the small town school paper which has shown the greatest improvement during the past year. Your courageous handling of a vital school problem will serve as an inspiration to the staffs of other school papers. May you continue the good work."

Applause met his last words. He raised his hand. "I want the staff of *Tattler* and their faculty adviser to step up to the platform."

Peggy felt numb standing before the assembly, and her hands were cold. *I don't belong here. I didn't do anything. I tried to fight it.*

It was later that day that the decision came to her. "You don't understand," she said to Miss Sands. "Besides . . ." She stopped herself. It wasn't Miss Sands' business that Grant had no use for her. "I want to resign. I'm not much good here, anyhow. Anyone can do proof."

Miss Sands was busy looking in her briefcase. She brought out a familiar-looking blue notebook. "I think these characterizations are delightful," she said.

Peggy's eyes widened. "Where . . . ? How did you . . . ?"

"Anne brought them to me. She believes in you. We all do, Peggy."

Except Grant, Peggy thought dolefully.

"I've been thinking," Miss Sands went on, "that you might do a weekly profile in the *Tattler*. Characterizations—like these."

Peggy felt herself beaming like an idiot. It was a wonderful idea. Why hadn't she thought of it? "Profiles of interesting students—of those who have unusual backgrounds or hobbies or . . ." She stopped as an idea came to her. "I'll have one for the next *Tattler*." She paused, held out her hand. "I've been awful, Miss Sands. You're swell." Then she hurried away, scarlet with embarrassment.

Live on your best side, Anne had said. The thought sat in the back of her mind as she pecked at her dad's typewriter. Two days later she handed Miss Sands a manuscript.

Peggy thrilled to it in print. Only Miss Sands was present when she handed Grant the corrected proof. "We have to fit this into the make-up," she said casually, her heart thumping. A second later she looked up to see Miss Sands closing the door behind her, smiling conspiratorially.

She waited breathlessly as he read it, noting the way his dark hair fell in a cowlick. Then suddenly he faced her, his eyes eloquent. He was gripping her arms, gathering her to him, kissing her. "Peggy . . ." his voice was rough. "I said such things to you. It was only because I cared."

She shushed him. "Let's forget the past." And as twilight darkened about them, "And let's get that proof back to the printer."

She read it again over his shoulder, feeling proud that she'd had the courage to write it.

Grant Dyke wants to be a newspaperman, and from the looks of things he'll make it. That famous editorial which won us the scholastic award has practically insured his winning the editorship of *The Tattler* next term. . . . You can be sure in that case that *Tattler* will be unique—for Grant Dyke is an individual in all things. He'll tell you almost belligerently that he dislikes baseball, but watch his enthusiasm for model airplanes, railroads and old Yankee clippers. He likes square dancing better than round and can sing you reams of American ballads. "Grant's voice is terrible," his apple-cheeked mother says, "but he makes up for it in sincerity." That's the keynote of Grant's character —the quality we all noticed working with him these past few weeks when he unstintingly jumped in to fill a staff vacancy and gave so much time and effort.

You probably didn't pay much attention—because Grant doesn't make much noise. He's quiet, likes sloppy clothes, good books. There's no flashy surface there. But he's just the kind of person who's contributed most to our world. We're proud to start our "Profile of the Week" with Grant Dyke. . . .

Her eyes trailed off the page, and she thought, I'll have to do one of Anne. . . .

When she and Grant left the office together, a slice of moon peeped from the orchid dusk. It was cold, but Peggy felt a warm contentment in her heart. "The Tambor?" she asked.

"Certainly, Peg: quality in all things—waffles, coffee, and you."

They smiled, linked arms, and headed against the wind.

A Night Filled with Music

D. V. S. JACKSON

KAREN was the only passenger in the creaky little elevator. She was impatient at its slowness, wanting it to hurry because it had taken her so long to get to this point. The day was here; her chance had come. She was frightened a little, but it was time she started; she was sixteen and a half. She was obsessed with a sense of hurry. She did not want to be old before she touched success.

The elevator halted and swung a little in its shaft, then let her out into a dim, shadowy, mean little hall with four closed doors leading off it. She picked out the door she wanted as the elevator squeaked down. There was the sound of a piano beating out measures and the thump of feet from behind it. She knocked. The piano stopped. The thumping stopped. Then the door was snatched open and a burst of warm sunlight splashed out at her, and she thought, suddenly, of a spotlight.

The man who opened the door stared at her. She smiled

back hesitantly, recognizing him from pictures she had seen. This was Igor, who made dancers. He did not smile back.

"I'm Karen Mueller," she said, nervously.

"Well . . ." he said. "Come, then." He moved away from the door and she walked into a room that was all sunlight from the windows and the overhead skylight. She was conscious of a group of dancing students lined up in class position, standing loosely, distracted by her entry. "So?" said Igor, as he closed the door.

"My ballet teacher wrote to you about me," she reminded him.

He shrugged wearily, as if that was always happening. "I see if I take you," he said. "Get dressed. In there."

The dressing room was an untidy closet, hung around with clothes on hooks and hangers. Overhead shelves spilled down possessions. Benches were loaded with boxes and luggage and shoes and umbrellas, and odd gear bulged from underneath.

There were two occupants in the tiny room, one a brassy blonde sitting on the only chair, smoking. She was dressed in black tights and her feet were stretched out before her, as if she were contemplating her pink satin toe shoes. The other was a slim, tiny girl, with long fair hair tied in a horsetail at the back with a black ribbon. This girl was sitting on a bench, putting on toe shoes. She smiled at Karen. "Are you a new pupil?" she asked.

"If I'm accepted," Karen said, and introduced herself.

"I'm Alice," the girl said. "That's Joyce."

Joyce stared at Karen through the smoke of her cigarette.

Alice went back to wrapping lambs' wool around her feet. Karen could not help watching with professional interest. *Her toes were too long*, she thought. The big toe was already bent in sharply, and the nails were bruise-blackened. Alice was pleasant, but not young. Twenty-three, maybe even older.

Karen swung her overnight bag up on a bench and began to change to practice clothes.

Alice said, wistfully, "You've got beautiful feet, Karen."

Karen looked down. They were dancers' feet, short, strong, with toes almost all the same length, steady as rocks for toe work.

". . . and little," Alice said. "What size shoe do you take?"

"Toe shoes? Size three," Karen said.

"That's what I take," Alice said.

Joyce got up abruptly, threw her cigarette in the sink, and stalked out. Karen turned back to Alice. "What kind of a teacher is Igor?" she asked.

"Wonderful, if you work hard," Alice said. "But he doesn't usually take beginners. Do you have any stage experience?"

"No," Karen admitted, "but I've been taking ballet after school hours since I was eight. I'm finished with high school now and can really concentrate on my dancing."

"You look strong," Alice said, finishing the knot on her ribbons, ". . . and that helps a lot." She stood up. "I have to go now. He only sent me in to change my shoes. Igor's strict. No lingering in the dressing room. No coming in late. No doubling classes with other teachers. You know." She opened the door. "Good luck," she said over her shoulder, and left.

Karen thought a moment of Igor. She had never had a man teacher, and it was strange to consider it. Igor had been dressed in a blue business suit, and his hair was graying. He did not look like a dancer; he was ordinary, except for his eyes. They were black and faceted, as if they wanted to hit out first. Remembering the eyes, Karen finished dressing hurriedly.

She was ignored when she came out of the dressing room, so she sat quietly on a bench near the piano and watched. It was pretty to see the class dancing in the sunlight. It was a double picture, too, because the entire front wall of the studio was one immense mirror, making twins of everyone.

"You!" came a voice, commanding. "Warm up!"

"Me?" she asked, uncertain.

"You think I talk to the bench?"

So she warmed up in a corner, out of the way of the class, and remembered how she had pleaded to come here. *Please, Pop, I only want to dance. I'll die if I can't.* And Pop saying how he had worked hard all his life to save money for her education, a doctor, a lawyer, anything she wanted. Mom saying, *she wants to dance, Karl, only to dance, and she needs her final training.* Pop saying no child of his would run around half naked on a stage . . . that was for immoral people. *Please, Pop, please!* Pop shaking his finger at Mom and saying, *she gets it from your side.* Mom getting mad and saying, *because my sister was a concert singer? Your mother played the organ every Sunday in the church* . . . and desperate; *please, Pop, please!*

"You . . ." yelled Igor, adding, ". . . with the red hair," so this time there would be no doubt. He pointed to the center of the floor.

She stepped out into the middle of the room. The class wandered off to the walls and sat down on the floor to rest, with towels around their necks, watching. Karen thought, this was a new world, this was not kid stuff, but a desperate contest, a struggle for success. And this time, Mom could not plead for her. It was herself, all alone.

Igor pulled a chair to the front of the room, by the mirror, and sat upon it backward, facing her. "Now," he said, "we see if you have two left feet."

During a class lesson, Igor walked restlessly around, circling the students, with a stick carried behind his back like a tail hanging down. "Long lines," he would keep saying. "You dance like crabs!" Then impatiently, "Straighten the knee!" Sometimes he would warn them twice, if he was in a good mood. After that he used the stick, hard.

The first week, Karen went home every night with welts on her legs and resentment inside. But then, she noticed the new sharpness in her dancing, a clarity the other teachers had never given her, and she forgave the stick, but always hated it and never overcame ducking whenever she heard a swish.

"Ha!" Igor would shout, if she dodged. "Guilty conscience!"

He was almost unbearably strict, but Karen knew why very soon. There was a spirit in the studio, the last lingering light of a great bright star called Eksterina Constantinova. The great Constantinova, who was dead even before Karen was born. The Constantinova who had been Igor's mother. When she found that out, Karen understood why Igor had a sort of scorn to his teaching, as if he knew they could never hope to be like Constantinova, and held it against them because not even a bit of the star dust sparkled on their heads. And they, feeling it dumbly, strove impossibly for what they could not reach, knowing that grand failure was a kind of success.

The great ballerina had been dead a long time, yet in the class they talked of her as if she still existed. It was Alice who resembled Constantinova, they all agreed, small and fair.

Joyce went further, adding, "She's the pet. She'll get the best because she looks like Constantinova. Us poor slobs will have to make our own breaks. I'll make mine, don't worry." Joyce always showed her teeth when she smiled; you were never sure it was a smile.

Karen hated to agree with Joyce, but the favoritism seemed so plain. For Alice there was always praise—for her lightness, her delicacy of motion, the beautiful poise. If Alice slowed down or looked tired, she was told to rest a while.

Karen tried very hard to catch up to Alice, to make up for her own immaturity by work. She would skip eating at lunchtime, so she could practice by herself in the empty studio, watching in the mirror, criticizing, trying steps again and again. Gradually the world would fade away and she would be whichever favorite ballerina she had seen last.

One day, suddenly, she saw Igor standing in the door of his office, watching. She stopped abruptly, startled, embarrassed. She did not know how long he had been there.

"You have it wrong," he said, instead of scolding. "Look, I show you."

After that, he watched her often from his doorway.

They had visitors to the studio very often, friends of Igor's mostly, sometimes men who wanted dancers for a show. Always Alice was asked to dance, because Igor liked to show her off, but never Karen. Never Joyce. Joyce did not seem to care; she stared unsmiling, like a tigress waiting. Some day she would leap, Karen knew, with her claws all spread, but not over a few steps in a class. Karen tried hard to be as patient, but she was nearly seventeen. It was harder to stand aside and wait. One day a certain man came. He had visited before, and Igor always treated him like royalty. This time, they talked Russian in a corner, and the man seemed to be explaining something, asking a favor and giving specifications, all at once.

When they stopped the secret conversation, Igor said, in English, "Now I show you my children." Three girls danced, and inevitably it was, "Alice . . . come."

He won't ask me to dance, Karen thought angrily, *but he can't stop me from practicing.* So she ground the toes of her shoes in the rosin box. And then she did turns.

Turns are like circus stunts, if the dancer wants them to be. Fireworks broke out in the corner as Karen did *grands fouettés.* The students ducked in all directions to avoid her flying foot. Her hair lashed out in a red cloud, and the gold cross she always wore sprang out the length of its chain.

"Karen!" she heard Igor bellow.

She stopped, clean, no staggering or imbalance, and put her feet in a demure fifth position, to show off her perfect balance.

Igor's eyes were black. "You go home now," he said. "You go home!"

"This one, too," the strange man said.

"No," Igor said. "She is the baby."

"The redhead too," the man insisted.

Igor spit out some fast Russian, and Karen lingered, trying to understand. Igor suddenly cracked her hard across the rear, and she squealed and leaped for the dressing room and fell in with a scramble before he got the stick.

It was wintry daylight when she came out into the street, and bitter cold. She did not dare go home so early to be questioned, so she wandered along Fifth Avenue.

She no longer felt confident. In the studio, she thought she must fight to get ahead, claw her way—but now she was uncertain. Uncertainty led to fright, that maybe she was *not* as good a dancer as she thought she was, as she wanted to be. If she only knew, if there was only a sign, she could do anything, stand anything, if only in her heart she was sure. She wandered on. Of course she would be a dancer, of course she would be on the stage. She began the old game of what she would call herself. Not Mueller, that was not a dancer's name. Something else, clear and simple, that would look good in lights. She favored Griffin, because it had the tang of antiquity to it. A griffin was a fabulous animal, and she would be a fabulous dancer; maybe as great as Constantinova—and then, discouraged, she recognized her daydreaming and put it away.

She was stiff with cold, but it was still too early to go home. She decided to look in at some of the classes other teachers held. Nobody minded if strangers looked on, for

often they were students shopping for a new teacher. It
would kill time and she would be out of the cold.

The subway was slow the next morning and she was late.
She opened the door quietly, hoping to sneak in, but it was
as if Igor was waiting for her. He stopped the class and
pounced.

"Miss Mueller," he said. He bowed, extravagantly. "Very
nice you come." He straightened up and his face was cruel.
"Now you turn around and go out again." He pointed.
"Go!"

"Go where?" she asked, bewildered.

"Didn't you pick out yesterday?" he demanded. He
named the studios where she had been, the classes she had
watched, backing her out into the hall as he moved toward
her. He slammed the door with fury, and left her standing
in the dark hall.

She walked about in Central Park all morning in the
cold.

At lunchtime, her feet carried her back to the studio. It
would be empty; Igor would be alone.

She went in, and the door to his office was closed now,
tightly. She swallowed and knocked softly.

"Come," he said, as if he was tired.

She pushed the door open. He was sitting at his desk,
writing, and all around the small room were framed pictures of dancers. He looked up.

"I didn't do anything yesterday," she said, hurriedly, "I
only went to those classes to get out of the cold. I didn't
even talk to anybody."

He put his pen on the desk and pushed back his chair.

"I didn't know you'd be mad," she said. "I didn't even
think you'd ever find out where I was."

"Find out!" he exclaimed. "After I brag about you to
everybody? They rush right to a phone to tell me you
shop for a new class. It is like you put a knife in my back."

She had never thought of any emotion but anger in Igor; never expected anything but sarcasm.

"I'm sorry," she said, awkwardly.

He turned a little and looked up at a picture. Of a girl in a long, old-fashioned classic skirt. "You think she learned in one day, like you want?" he asked.

"Is that . . . is that . . ."

"Yes," he said, turning back to Karen. "That is Constantinova."

"My mother saw her dance once," Karen said. "Before I was born. My mother said it was in Paris, in France. She went to visit my aunt, and they went to the ballet. My mother said she saw Constantinova only that once, and . . . she never forgot."

"That was a little before she died maybe," Igor said. "She was all tired then. My mother was brave, but she had a hard life. When the revolution came in Russia, they shot my father, and we ran away. I was only eleven, no help, only a worry. We got to Riga, then to France. She danced there. She died there." He stopped abruptly, as if he did not want to talk about it any more.

The door to the studio from the hall slammed. The students were coming for the next class. Igor called for Alice and Joyce to come in. Then he told the three that the man who had come to the studio the day before had a ballet troupe, a good one. He needed a soloist. Three of them were picked to do a variation during a ballet; that was the way the man worked. He wanted to see them before an audience, but in a small part so they could not do too much damage. Then the best of the three would do a very little solo near the end of the ballet, and be picked to stay with the troupe.

Alice glowed all over. This was why she had left a good corps de ballet job to take more training, to fit herself for a soloist's place. Joyce said nothing. Nor did Karen.

Alice asked when, and Igor told them, and something

inside of Karen hopped all around. Maybe it was her heart. Because the date was her seventeenth birthday. And to do the solo was the gift she wanted most, the gift she would give to herself!

The time went very fast; learning the steps was a joy. The day came, and they were dismissed before lunch, to go home and rest before the performance. There would be no birthday meal today, Karen thought, because she could not eat much before she danced, but it was worth losing her seventeenth birthday. Mom and Pop felt bad, but to Karen it was nothing, compared with tonight. Tonight!

Karen dressed faster than the others, and went ahead of them into the hall. She pressed the elevator button.

And then Igor was beside her. "Karen," he said, "I have to tell you, do not be disappointed."

"I won't be afraid," she said. "I've been in recitals."

"I know, I know," he said, and took her arm. "What I mean to say is, this place is for Alice. You understand? You know what I mean?" he asked, anxiously.

"I know," she said, and all the things Joyce said came back. *He doesn't want me to do my best and win over his pet. He doesn't want me to do my best.* It was—betrayal. "I understand," she said, and pulled her arm away from him with a jerk. The elevator opened its door and she stepped in.

"Karen?" he said.

She would not turn around until the elevator was creaking down. She felt cold and hard inside, the way Joyce looked sometimes.

Alice went first up the narrow iron stairs to the stage level, Joyce was second, and Karen came up last, warily, seeing her enemies before her. Their long, white, tulle skirts filled up all the space in the stairway, like clouds floating upward. Karen thought of the stage then. She had practiced on it before the empty seats and knew every crack and splinter, every unevenness. It was a wicked stage. It had a sharp slope built into it, so that it slid down toward the orchestra pit. It was made to display singers and cripple dancers. When you turned, you had to pull back sharply or lose your balance. It would be so easy to misjudge. . . . She left that thought precipitately. She would be all right.

There was turmoil around the stage when they approached from the wings, people dragging things, a man ordering other people. Karen dug her feet in a box of rosin.

Then she heard music, beyond the curtain. And suddenly, it hit her hard. *She had to go out on that stage and dance in front of people!* Her mouth went dry. Frantically, she tried to recall her steps to reassure herself. She could not remember; it was the way it was in high school, before she took her finals. She felt hot, then cold; next, she began to sweat. She was cold all over and she felt nauseous.

The ice cream and cake, she thought. Mom had insisted on that at lunch, the semblance of a birthday party, so she would not miss everything, and now the rich cake and the ice cream and the candy were battling inside.

She saw Igor and looked away, but he came over to her anyway. He ran a finger across her collarbone and looked at it, gleaming wet.

"Nerves," he said. "Good. You learn respect for the audience." Then he put his arm lightly around her waist. "Karen, baby," he said, "take care of Alice for me, yes?" He gave her a quick pat and went over to Alice.

Then they took their positions on the stage. The extra people all dashed off. The three of them posed like statues, with blank faces. It was a white ballet, and they had been warned sternly not to mug at the audience. There were twelve other dancers on the stage, but Karen felt all alone.

The curtain rose slowly, smoothly. It was too late to run now. The music sounded louder with the barrier gone. The footlights were small suns, blinding. Karen could see nothing but the dancers at the front of the stage, blacked into silhouettes. But beyond them was the Audience. There was no noise, but they were there, breathing and watching, and Mom and Pop among them. The unheard sound of all the people breathing pounded, rising and falling, until at last Karen understood it was her own heart, the blood singing in her ears. She tried desperately to remember the music, the steps, her cue, but she could not.

There was a slight hesitation in the music. It was familiar for no reason at all, and responding to a stimulus she did not recognize, she jumped up on her toes, and then it all came back.

And when they were still again, being statues, after the bit they had danced, her stomach-ache was gone, and she could see beyond the lights, bits and pieces of the audience. A flash of light on eyeglasses. The red "Exit" signs. Hear a cough up in the balcony.

Beside her, Alice sighed a little.

"What's the matter?" Karen asked, barely moving her lips.

"I think I have a splinter in my foot," Alice said. "I hit it against some scenery."

"When Joyce crowded you?" Karen had seen it. "If she tries to make you move faster than the music again," Karen advised, "kick back at her. She'll move away."

Alice's arm touched Karen's and she was trembling. Karen looked down. One of Alice's pink toe shoes was splotched with red stains.

"Is it all right?" Alice asked. Her fluffy skirt prevented her from seeing her own feet, Karen thought, which was lucky. She remembered the time Alice had cut her finger and fainted.

"They're fine," Karen said. "Just keep your head up."

Alice's face was white under the make-up.

Karen turned her head slowly in the other direction and looked out of the corner of her eye. Joyce was smiling a little.

"Leave her alone," Karen said.

"You're next," Joyce said.

It was like two tigresses meeting head-on in a path where there was only room for one.

Yet when they moved a little on the stage, Joyce still pursued Alice. Karen watched helplessly as Joyce flashed brilliant dancing, imperceptibly not giving Alice enough room, or crowding her so she landed off balance. Alice was all nerves, she would be driven too far, she did not know how to protect herself, she was too gentle. Only her spirit, her talent fought for her. But Joyce was driving her beyond her endurance.

Karen tried to help, she tried to stay between them, knowing it was dangerous, remembering Joyce had said, *you're next*. She did her steps, remembering how she must move, tried to help Alice, and at the same time tried to see how Joyce would plot, when Joyce would try to injure her.

On cue, the lights of the stage were dimming, dimming . . . the three young dancers were to leap behind a stage prop and kneel down, hidden . . . and then Karen knew what Joyce had planned.

Alice leaped in lightly, and sank down on her injured foot. The lights were lower. Karen leaped in. The lights were almost out, the orchestra was storming. Joyce leaped in, trying to hit Karen's feet, coming down hard. But Karen had shoved over hard, just as Joyce leaped. She had spared herself the worst; she got kicked on the instep, but Joyce had missed her ankle. They crouched in the dark for a second.

Karen did not see Igor. She heard Joyce struggle suddenly, and the sound of dragging. When the lights came up, she looked offstage, and Joyce was being shoved off. Igor had one arm twisted behind her, and his other hand was over her mouth so she could not yell.

"What happened?" asked Alice, bewildered, seeing there were only two of them.

"Joyce left," Karen said, rubbing her foot. She had a dirt mark on her tights, and underneath it hurt. She would have a nasty bruise.

"What will we do?" Alice asked.

"What we're supposed to do," Karen said. "Dance." She did not mean to be glad, but she was all right, she would be able to dance the solo; and Alice could go no further.

Karen and Alice did *pas de bourrées* offstage, and one of them was through for the night. The other would have a few minutes of rest—and then—the little solo! Karen breathed hard, to catch her breath, to have enough wind for it.

Igor had shoved a chair under Alice and was cutting the ribbons of the shoe that was bloody. "Don't look down!" he was ordering her, knowing how she might faint. "Karen!" he said then, and she stood ready. "Your feet are the same size. Take off your shoe for Alice . . . hurry. Why do you stand?"

"Take off my shoe?"

"Yes, yes . . . hurry, now. I do not have all day."

"Wait a minute," the man who had visited the studio said. "You were right about Joyce. I don't want any trouble-maker in my troupe; and this one can't dance. Let the red-head do the solo."

Karen held her breath.

"No," said Igor positively. "Alice can dance it, only with another shoe. See, a little tape over the cut, a new shoe— she can dance."

Igor was tying the ribbons of Karen's shoe around Alice's ankle, and the dream was over. There was no place for her here, Karen thought. She walked away, her head high, so no one would think she had wanted to dance the solo. On two feet she was not as good as Alice on one. That had been Igor's judgment, and he made dancers. She could not bear it, inside. She had wanted only to dance; and to have the desire, but not the ability, to transmit desire to reality, that was beyond human endurance. As long as she lived, she would never forget her seventeenth birthday. She would hate it all her life.

She went down the iron stairs with her tulle skirt fluffed out under the railing, one foot naked on the cold iron.

Then from behind her she could hear a music cue. The birthday gift she had promised for herself. It was the cue for the little solo at the end of the ballet. Karen sat down slowly on the iron stairway. Her skirt blew softly in the drafts of air, like wisps of white fog. Beautiful music, rising from the orchestra, then bending like a fountain to sprinkle shimmering notes on the audience and dancers.

But the night would never be filled with music for her. Her eyes filled with hot tears.

The iron stairs shook a little. She did not look up, until she felt something hit her shoulders. She saw Igor's feet. He had taken off his coat and thrown it over her. "You get stiff in the draft," he said, severely. She shoved the coat off her shoulders.

He put it back. "Leave it!" he said. He sat down on the step above her, and pushed her skirt over so he could get his feet down. He bent over and touched the mark on her foot, and she pulled her foot away. "It will be all right," he said, as he straightened up. Then, "Alice will be happy here. The ballerinas are young and will do the hard work. Alice will never have to dance too much, but the people will see her. She should not be lost because she is not strong."

Karen could not talk because it would choke her.

"Do you feel bad?" he asked. "Look, I will show you your name in the program." He held it out in front of her. She wanted to thrust it away angrily, to say she would not be second best, she would not waste Pop's money on that; but she could not. She had to look just once because it was like an obituary chiseled on a stone: *Here lies Karen Mueller. She died young.*

With the tears in her eyes, she could not find the name. Mueller—no. It must be listed as Griffin. But she could not find that either. She wiped her eyes furtively.

"Here," said Igor. He stuck his finger under a name. She had to look and look again, before she realized whose name it was. *Karen Constantinova*, it read.

"But Alice . . ." she said. "But Alice . . . looked like her."

"Oh, a little," he said. "On the outside."

And she remembered then something that Igor had said once, that the great dancers did not pass on their creative ability to the children of their body, but often to pupils. The inheritance was by the spirit, not the flesh.

So she put her head down in her hands and she cried. Constantinova. It was such a long name, and no one would ever pronounce it right, but there was no other she would have wanted. It was a symbol, and a promise, and a goal. It was all the faith Igor had in her future; the first light on what was to come.

The stairs were quaking under her. Someone was at the top, but she could not stop crying. She kept her face hidden.

"Hey, how about you two moving over so a guy can get down?" some man asked.

"Go another way," Igor replied, imperiously. "She is too tired to move."

"She can be tired some place else then," the man said roughly. "I got to get downstairs."

"You don't get down these stairs," Igor said, "unless I throw you down." His voice was hard and threatening.

The man swore and stamped away muttering.

"Some day you will tell about it," Igor shouted after him. "How you couldn't get down the stairs because Karen Constantinova was sitting on them. Some day you will *brag!*"

One Fainting Robin

DOROTHY WITTON

WHEN VALERY opened her eyes and saw the group at the foot of her hospital bed, she knew that they were discussing her again—Dad and Mother and Dr. Sullivan. They were holding another of their endless, worried consultations on how to drag her back to a life she did not want.

Why couldn't they just let her alone, she thought wearily. She closed her eyes, hoping to escape once more into sleep. But her mother saw she had wakened and came to the head of the bed.

"Had a little nap, didn't you, darling?" she asked, her voice too brightly cheerful. "How do you feel this afternoon?"

Valery turned her head, trying not to see the yearning pity so thinly disguised by determined optimism. She knew they were trying to help her, and she wanted to be grateful. But it was as though she existed on another planet. All their efforts to establish contact were useless.

"I'm all right," she said, trying to manage a smile. "What have you three been secretly plotting now?"

She noticed, indifferently, the quick exchange of glances among them. Her father came to the other side of the bed.

"It's pretty hard to do any secret plotting around a smart girl like you!" he said with elaborate playfulness. Then he dropped that tone and continued gently, "Honey, don't you want us to get a tutor for you soon, so that you can begin making up some of your school work? Now that the cast is off, and you're not in pain any more—" He looked at her hopefully.

Perhaps not the kind of pain you mean, thought Valery. Physical pain was the least of the torture she suffered. Physical pain was almost welcome, since it kept her from thinking too much about the other kind.

"Or if you don't want a tutor yet," her mother put in, "why don't you try the occupational therapy that Dr. Sullivan suggested? They have a lovely place upstairs."

Valery moved her head restlessly, feeling smothered by their anxiety. If only they wouldn't try so hard!

Her mother put a pleading hand on her arm. "It's just to help you convalesce more rapidly, Val. Dr. Sullivan says you aren't pulling out of the last operation as quickly as you should."

Valery looked at Dr. Sullivan, standing at the foot of the bed. It was nice of him to worry about her, she thought remotely. To him she must be just another "case." He had done his best as a surgeon. Why couldn't he just let it go at that?

"Later perhaps, Mother," she promised numbly. Anything to end the torture, for the moment. "When I feel a little stronger. I think I could sleep a little more now."

After they had left, looking defeated and a little hurt, Valery stared lifelessly at the ceiling. Why, why, why had this cruel thing happened to her?

She knew what Dr. Sullivan thought: that she was not

trying to get well. And it was true. Why should she? Life was over, nipped in the bud. She had felt nothing but bitter despair that day after the last operation, when she had heard her wardmates whispering, thinking she was too ill to hear: "Poor girl—crippled for life—so young—pretty, too."

The horror of those whispered words had been with her ever since, like a living nightmare. Even when her anguished parents had tried to reassure her, it made no difference. She would not be bedridden, they told her. One leg would be shorter than the other, the knee a little stiff. She would have a slight limp. And the scars on her face would disappear in time. Before long, she would be as pretty as ever.

But never again to run on two strong legs. Never again to dance, to play tennis, to swim—

She turned to stare out of the window. The gray February twilight was already closing in, but there was still light enough to see the snow-covered slope beyond the hospital, the barren trees. That was the kind of world that awaited her if she recovered—forever frozen, dreary, and cold.

She closed her eyes, remembering the October afternoon four months ago—the day before the accident. It was as though, because of the horror that followed it, the details of that beautiful day were stamped forever on her brain.

It had been an Indian-summer afternoon, warm enough for shorts, yet with a tang in the air. The maple trees around the tennis courts were a riot of vivid red and orange, almost unbearably beautiful.

She and Quint had played three hard sets and then, lounging on the grass, had talked for an hour about what they meant to do with their lives. A great happiness welled up in her, partly from the hard exercise of her own strong body and partly from the look in Quint's eyes when he said, "Sure, physical education is a good field for you, Val.

For a while at least. It'll probably be useful training for the wife of a guy who may be sent all over the globe." Quint was planning to be a construction engineer.

Walking home later, through a twilight that smelled of burning leaves, they heard a piano from an open window: a series of runs, liquid and sweet like a fountain rising and falling. Quint took her hand and said only, "Valery?" There was no need to answer.

That late afternoon had held all joy and promise. Valery had felt there was no dream too impossible to realize. She was Valery Mason, the prettiest and most popular girl in her class, the best all-around girl athlete. Quint cared for her, and the world was in the palm of her hand.

Then, the next morning, the terrifying collision had happened. It had turned the world upside down and brought her to this hospital, shattered and broken.

At first, the doctors had been hopeful. But now, after three operations and various complications, they admitted themselves defeated. Her left leg would never be the same.

Valery stared bitterly at the ceiling again. How could Mother and Dad, with all their sympathy, know what it was like to be strong and beautiful one day, scarred and crippled the next? How could they imagine what it was to have seen Quint's eyes, admiring and tender in October, full of pity and horror in December?

He had come to visit her just once, before Christmas. The bandages were still on her face then; one arm and both legs were incased in plaster. She had received him coldly and had seen his relief when she had discouraged him from coming again.

She would have refused all visitors if Dr. Sullivan had permitted it. He insisted company was good for her, and had recommended a four-bed ward instead of a private room. But it made little difference. Valery hardly noticed her roommates, most of whom were convalescent cases, coming and going quickly.

"Hi, Valery, here's your supper." The nurse's aid expertly flipped up the table leaf with one hand and swung it over the bed. "Shall I crank your bed up a little higher?"

"Thanks, this is all right."

For a long time she stared dully at the food she did not want—the food that would keep her alive.

When Miss Luffington, the night nurse came in for the bedtime ritual of back-rubbing and bed-straightening, she said brightly, "There'll be a new doctor tomorrow, Valery. Not new to the hospital, but he's been away since you've been here. You'll like Dr. Pritchard."

Valery shrugged indifferently. Another doctor was nothing exciting, she thought drearily. There had already been too many of them.

But when Dr. Pritchard dropped in the next morning, Valery would never have guessed he was a doctor but for his white hospital coat with the two horns of a stethoscope sticking up from one pocket. He was deformed. His neck seemed to be deeply sunken between enormous, high shoulders from which his body tapered to extremely thin legs. He looked top-heavy. But his face—Valery looked again at his face. This was the first time in four months that she had given a second look at anything, and even then she could not have said what it was that drew her.

His features were in no way extraordinary, but the expression in his gray eyes was so intense that Valery had the feeling that he already knew everything there was to know about her. Not just her case history, but what went on inside of her.

"Hello," he said quietly. "I'm Dr. Pritchard."

Valery inclined her head, waiting for the usual cheerful questions.

But Dr. Pritchard was looking out the window. When he turned back to her, he said abruptly, "They tell me you were a fine all-around athlete. Tough break."

Valery sucked in her breath. Was this a new kind of

"shock treatment?" No one had mentioned sports to her for four months.

"Yes," she said stiffly. "I was going to be a physical-education teacher."

He grunted. "Well, now you'll have to be something else. What sport do you like best?"

She did not answer for a moment. Then she said, "I liked swimming best. I held the city record in backstroke."

He nodded. "You'll still be able to swim, of course, but you probably won't break any more records. I swim, myself."

He stared out of the window again, suddenly seeming wistful. Valery looked furtively at his misshapen body. Then, without intending to, she gave him a dose of his own medicine: "What sport would you have preferred?"

He grinned at her. "The ambition of every male weakling. Football. I always played halfback in my dreams."

Valery answered his smile with her own. And they talked for fifteen minutes—about sports!

After he had gone she felt let down, suspicious, as though she had been betrayed into confidences. Probably this was a new kind of therapy, she thought. And yet, for the first time in weeks, she felt herself in contact with another human being.

Dr. Pritchard came every day after that, to chat for a little while. Almost without realizing it, Valery began to look forward to his visits. She wakened in the morning with a faint stirring of hope, instead of the horror and dread of another empty day.

They talked about all kinds of things. He did not skirt subjects that might be painful to her. And perhaps for that very reason there was no unbridgeable gulf between them. He always managed to convey the impression that he had unlimited time for these social visits with her, although Valery learned from the nurses that he was a very busy man.

Several times, Dr. Pritchard had glanced with interest at

the array of books around Valery's bed, gifts from her parents and friends. One morning he picked up a volume entitled *Poems of Emily Dickinson.*

"What do you think of this?" he asked.

"I haven't read it," Valery confessed. "I've hardly read at all since I—"

He was plainly shocked. "All this beautiful leisure—and you're not reading these fine books!" he exclaimed. "If I could just have two hours of your day—"

"I'd gladly give you all of it," Valery said grimly. Then, as she spoke, she realized that what she had said was not quite true.

"Don't be foolish," he went on. "Someday, when you're involved with a profession or a family—or both—you'll give your eyeteeth to have a few of these precious hours for reading."

"Not me," she said positively. To herself she added, "Because I won't be involved with either a profession or a family."

But after he had gone, she picked up the volume and began leafing through it. Suddenly she was reading intently. When the dinner trays arrived, she was still absorbed.

How many things there were in that slender book that seemed to ring a bell inside of her! One in particular, she kept going back to:

> If I can stop one heart from breaking,
> I shall not live in vain;
> If I can ease one life the aching,
> Or cool one pain,
> Or help one fainting robin
> Into his nest again,
> I shall not live in vain.

"That must be the way Dr. Pritchard feels," she whispered to herself. "And I am the fainting robin—or I was!"

She knew now that Dr. Pritchard's "treatment" was altering her outlook on life. She no longer wanted to die.

A few nights later a serious case was brought into her ward, and Valery had an opportunity to see Dr. Pritchard in action. The patient was a thin Polish woman who spoke little English. Her two English-speaking sons had accompanied her to the hospital and were allowed to come back after the nurses had completed their routine care.

The woman sat bolt upright in bed, staring straight ahead, her face flushed with fever. She was obviously very ill, but she was also terrified. The boys stood beside her, murmuring reassurances in Polish, but it could plainly be seen that they were unhappy about leaving her there.

When Dr. Pritchard came in, Valery saw his keen eyes take in the situation quickly. "You boys wait across the hall for a bit," he said gently. Quickly he swung the white curtains around the patient's bed.

Valery's already high opinion of Dr. Pritchard went up by leaps and bounds as she listened to him working behind the curtains. He knew a few words of Polish, and he used them all to put the little foreign lady at ease. He was infinitely patient, infinitely gentle, in his examination. His voice, as well as his words, constantly assured her that she was among friends.

After fifteen minutes, he pulled the curtains back. "Now I'm not going to bother you any more for a while," he said. "I'll send your boys in to say good night as soon as the nurse gives you something for that pain."

The woman lay back, her face relaxed, and her sons looked greatly relieved when they saw her.

"Your mother's going to be fine," Dr. Pritchard said. "You can come back in the morning. I'll get you a visiting permit." Valery saw the expression of gratitude on their faces as the two youths went out.

Sometime after midnight, she wakened to see Dr. Pritchard standing near the woman's bed, while a nurse held a flashlight for him. They were giving her a hypodermic and checking on the bottle and hose equipment for her intravenous feedings.

In the deep quiet of the hospital night, the scene had a weird, dramatic quality; and Valery lay thinking about it after they had gone. Then an idea burst upon her like a thunderclap. Why couldn't she be a nurse?

She would have only a slight limp, the doctors had said. Sick people wouldn't care about that. After the first five minutes no one, sick or well, thought about Dr. Pritchard's outward appearance. It was what he had inside of him that counted.

Toward morning she fell asleep with a little smile of contentment on her face.

During the weeks that followed, Dr. Pritchard was unusually busy, but Valery was patient. She knew that she no longer needed him so desperately. She could wait.

It was nearly Easter when he had time to hear her plans. He listened attentively as she spoke.

"That would be a fine thing for you, Valery," he said when she had finished. "You realize, of course, that there's little glamour about nursing. Some of it is sheer drudgery. Much of it is grim routine under stern discipline. But there are wonderful compensations."

"I know," she said humbly. "But if I could help only one person to begin to live again, as you have helped me, I'd consider it worth while."

"I'm proud of that tribute, Valery," he said quietly. "And I know you'll make a good nurse."

Easter Sunday was warm and bright. Yellow sunshine slanted across the white beds of the ward. Through the partly opened windows, earthy odors of spring and the call of birds breathed hope into the hospital.

On the slope beyond Valery's window, a single cherry

tree was in full bloom. She was enjoying its loveliness when her parents came.

"We brought you an Easter present, darling," her mother said. "Everybody is dressing up for Easter—" Then she hesitated. She knew that Valery had changed in the last few weeks, but she was not quite sure how much.

Valery opened the big box, lifting out a lovely pale blue robe.

"Mother! Dad!" she cried. "It's beautiful!" Delighted, they helped her slip it on.

"I have a gift for you, too," she told them. "The robe is just what I needed to show it off."

Lowering her feet carefully to the floor, she adjusted a pair of crutches, which she took from behind the curtains of her bed. Slowly but triumphantly she rose to her feet, then hobbled to the door and back.

Her mother burst into happy tears and her father blew his nose vigorously. Valery stood smiling at them.

"I'm ready for that tutor now," she said softly. "By July I'll be ready for summer school—without crutches. I have to study hard because after I graduate I'm going into training as a nurse!" There was a new determination and a kind of wonder in her voice.

"Val!"

"Don't cry now, Mom!" Valery said. Then she added, "You've both been so patient with me. I was a terrible coward, but—I'm going to make you proud of me yet."

She looked at the volume of Emily Dickinson beside her bed and lifted her eyes to the miracle of the blossoming cherry tree.

How could I ever have wanted to die, she thought incredulously. There is so much to live for!

Passing for
Herself

ISABEL KILCRIN

THE ROOM was still with the flat stillness of a place in which life constantly moves. The blackboards had been erased and washed, their dark surfaces left shining, smooth and bare. Fresh chalk lay in unbroken pieces between the dusted erasers.

The only sounds in the room were those of slow uncertain typing, occasional sighing, and a thin swish of wind pushing the paper forward in the machine. At another time it might have been pleasant to be alone in the room, Milly thought. But with the hopeless task with which she was confronted, her isolation was far from pleasant.

Why, she wondered, had she let herself be persuaded that she could do it? When Mr. Smith had stopped her on Wednesday and asked her to go to the town meeting to take notes, why had she felt proud rather than doubtful? Whatever had made her think she could do it?

"It'll be good experience for you, Milly," he had said.

"You just show 'em that we turn out good stenographers in the Junior as well as in the Senior class here in Milton High." He had started to walk away but had turned back. "If you do a good job, you'll get paid for it," he said. He was Office Practice instructor and she had found it flattering to be chosen out of a class of fifty-two.

I wonder why he did choose me? she thought dismally.

There were no voices now, nor any noises to distract her, but her work went at a snail's pace. She would not get paid for it; that much was certain. What impossible conceit had made her think she could do it? She had not known any of the men at the meeting and Mr. Hamilton had simply said: "The Messrs. Paul Smith, John Green, Richard Jones." Only not those names, of course. Nothing so simple. Their names had been strange sounding, like "J. Charles Montague" and "Vincent Pinwhitter" and "Atherton Presby" (or was it Presby Atherton? she worried). She had no idea to whom the names belonged. He'd said them just like that, one after another, expecting her to take them down and keep them straight as each man spoke. A miracle! If she could have done it!

The breeze blew a single sheet of paper off the desk. Sighing, she bent to pick it up. She looked at it ruefully, imagining the horrified reactions of the men to her report. She had lived in Milton almost two years but she had not met many of the older townspeople. As a result, she had been unable to tell the first selectman from the second. (There was a second, she felt reasonably sure; and perhaps a third and a fourth, but about that she was less certain.) In any case, they had all looked alarmingly alike. They had all sounded alarmingly alike. And they had all spoken alarmingly alike, a confused jumble of words with which she was almost totally unfamiliar, with only a small insignificant phrase here and there that she could grasp to reassure herself that they were not speaking in foreign tongues!

I hope Mr. Smith won't ask to see the report! she thought, wrinkling her forehead over her notes. I'll mail it out as soon as it's done. I'll say I'm sorry but I didn't keep a copy. And he'll say, "I told you to." Then I'll say, "I'm sorry, but I didn't understand."

Liar, she thought, continuing to study the baffling marks, feeling guilty and completely lost. Lies were not nice things. But what could she do? For a girl with the ability she was supposed to have, her ignorance was amazing. The truth was that even now she did not know what it had all been about. To save her life she could not name the topic of discussion. They might have been talking about a dam or bridge, or the digging of a ditch or road or something on or through or over town property! Or it might not have been town property. Perhaps the town was trying to buy the property, perhaps that was what it was all about.

Yes, because that would seem to fit in with the time that Mr. Somebody's son, the very good-looking young man with the red hair, had gotten up and stood proudly beside his father and said, very quietly, "I stand beside my father and beside my father's property." He had looked both noble and formidable, like a football hero, she thought. That was one sentence that was right. "I stand beside my father and beside my father's property." She hadn't missed *his* words. But who was his father? And who was this young man?

Who?

There was not the tiniest miraculous whisper in her head, informing her who he was. Yet she thought vaguely that his name was Hornsby, although why she thought so she could not tell. But, yes, it was Hornsby. She was sure of it.

It had been hot in the hall, and the men had puffed at pipes and cigars and cigarettes so that the air had been blue and gray, threaded with coiling smoke. When she had entered, Mr. Hamilton, the banker with the big nose and bushy eyebrows, had greeted her and shaken her hand quite limply for all his great size. He was chairman and he had looked at her sharply, even disapprovingly.

"Girl from the high school, are you?" he'd said, puffing out his lower lip formidably. "Certainly hope you're better than the last one they sent us. Made us wonder what we were paying taxes for! You look pretty young," he said. "Sit down." And he had shoved out a chair from a small table in the corner.

How old, she wondered, did he think a high school girl should look? Forty? With gray hair and wrinkles?

The chair had wobbled, one leg evidently shorter than the others, and she had seen the men through a haze of smoke and ignorance that added up to uncertain motion, rather like seasickness.

"I'm—not very experienced I'm afraid," she had admitted shakily, looking up at Mr. Hamilton appealingly. "This is my first year at stenographic work, you know. And I don't know who the men are."

"I asked them to send us a *good* girl," Mr. Hamilton snapped irritably, glancing at her doubtfully as he rapped on the desk. "Jed Lawton! Gentlemen!" he said in an annoyed tone. "The young lady from the high school is here and wants to know who you are. Will you please line up and look this way so I can tell her and she can write down your names? What is *your* name, young lady?" he said, turning to her.

"Mildred Benton."

"H'm!" He looked at her quizzically. "Don't know's I ever heard the name here. Well!"

She blushed, unable to account for his ignorance, feeling that all the men were smiling, laughing, and staring at her, most of them a little disinterestedly though, as if she should not have been so brown and square and slim, with straight dark hair and no perceptible curves under the sweater, and a family that nobody had ever heard of. She sat at the small table, embarrassed by the constant wobbling of the chair, and Mr. Hamilton began. "Jedidiah Lawton, first selectman; the Messrs. Malcolm Haley, Vincent Pinwhitter, Hamnet Hornsby—yes, that's right, girl, Hamnet Hornsby. Claims he's a descendant of Shakespeare. H'm . . . J. Charles Montague, John Wetherbee, Ned Adams . . . Am I going too fast?"

He was going much too fast and Milly knew names should never be taken down in shorthand unless they were very familiar ones, but she pushed the pencil over the paper desperately, trying to look capable, like a court stenographer, wondering how many names she would remember and how right she would get them. Hamnet Hornsby. Could he be the football hero's father?

Yes, she thought, deciding again for some evasive reason that he was. Still, she'd failed to get many names right, so the red-headed young man might very well be the son of Vincent Pinwhitter or Presby Atherton, for all she knew.

She pushed her chair back from the desk and walked to the window, tired of struggling with the problem, and there, outside, the silver green grass bent in the wind. Walt Whitman's "long uncut hair of graves," she thought. And, oh, how good it would be to be out there now! To lie in the windy grass and look at the sky and forget the wretched symbols in the notebook; to lie in the grass and dream. She wanted to go out, out, out—into the soft May air. And she knew that she must stay where she was and work a miracle.

A miracle, she reflected, was all that would do it. Positively. So why waste her time?

She knew the answer to that and sighed and fidgeted, her head quite empty. A fine state of affairs on Saturday morning! There was not another person in the whole school except Miss Altonbee, busily typing reports in the office. The steady tap-tap of the distant typewriter sounded like the thrum of a woodpecker, provocative, urging her to go out and accept the invitation of the lovely day. Still, the report was a duty, an obligation incurred, one that she could not drop. She must at least make a conscientious effort to do her best.

She went back to the desk and looked at her notes, sitting on the edge of the chair so that her bare legs rested against the frame of the desk and pressed against the smooth wood, making ridges in the flesh of her knees. She felt that she needed to lean hard against the desk for support, almost as though the harder she pressed, the more sure she would be of staying where she was and finishing her work.

Sighing, she turned again to the typewriter. She must at least type the thing and see if it added up to any kind of sense. And if it didn't to her, there was always the chance that it might to them, she decided.

Ordinarily, she thought, she could do better than she had done at the meeting. But she had been beaten from the start when a queer unpredictable feeling of panic had seized her and she'd been ashamed to admit it but had clutched at a word here, a sentence there. Yes, she had known with dreadful certainty during the meeting that the report would be a failure, and she had looked at the open door longingly, and had seen Sue Martin come swinging down the street on her bike. Then she had wished desperately to be outside, too, careless and free on her own bike in the soft spring air.

As the meeting progressed, things had gone rapidly from bad to worse. In the beginning the men had carried on their discussions rather slowly, in normal voices at normal rates of speed; but as they began to get excited, they had spoken faster, louder. In each case when a man wished to speak he had first to be recognized by the chairman. Then he rose and occasionally glanced her way or smiled and repeated a word that he thought might be unfamiliar to her, and Milly knew they all thought that she was getting it, whereas what she actually had when she came to transcribe her notes was all more or less like the first paragraph, a paragraph that added up to nothing at all!

She read it again:

"Mr. Chairman, Gentlemen,

"John Wetherbee (?) has told you tonight that the strip of land extending south from (blank) to the site of Miller's factory on the green at Kent (?) Place and the intersection, a matter of two and a half square miles, is absolutely essential for (blank). Still, Mr. Hornsby (?) Presby (?) refuses to sell, as I understand it, for less than eighteen thousand dollars on the grounds that he holds this (blank, blank, blank). Now this particular piece of land in question (blank) muddy, useless and (blank) . . ."

And even about that much, she thought, there were questions! He might have said "two and a half" or he might have said "ten and a half." He might have said "square miles" or just "miles." It was a puzzle, all right, and most of the parts were missing. Bridge, ditch, or road? Which?

The next part, she decided, sounds like a bridge. Yes, I'm sure it must be . . . I *think* . . .

"The straining action in the (blank) with a load at the extreme end, the bending (blank) may be represented by a triangle whose (blank) depth at the supports where obviously the intensity is represented by a (blank) whose depth equals (blank) ."

Oh, rats! she thought, this can't possibly make sense to anyone. It can't possibly! Those were actually blank spaces between the words, blank spaces where a few unimportant words or the most important words of all should go! And where would she get the correct words to put there if she didn't know what they were? Answer: she wouldn't.

"I stand beside my father and beside my father's property." Horrible, really, that one intelligible sentence, complete and coherent, in the midst of rubble and ruin! That one intelligible sentence . . .

She saw again the young man's face and her heart lurched, faintly but delightfully. There was something about the precise yet soft way his lips had gone together, she remembered, that had made her wonder how they would feel against her cheek! *He* would read the report, too! Oh, miserable!

Unhappily she struggled on, the confusing hodgepodge growing worse by the minute. Why must she try? Why type words on paper that would add up to nothing when she had done? Yet she must do it. She must type the words and send them to Mr. Hamilton with a copy to Mr. Lawton, and she must do it now.

Her whole being rebelled. Look out the window, she thought, just for a minute! Yet she resisted for she knew what lay outside: the delightful, the lovely day, still quite early morning. But her eyes refused to stay on the baffling notes. They fled their task and sought the framed motto over the door which, she thought, she must have read at least a thousand times that morning: "We pass for what we are." Emerson.

This time the words stopped her. Suddenly she thought she knew exactly what they meant. No matter what you do, what you *are* shows through, she thought. If your actions are false, in one way or another you show it. No one can be more than the sum of his days on earth, and no one can entirely hide it. It comes out in laughter or frowns, speech or silence. It shows in the way you walk, dress, act, your hands, and—most of all—in your face. Look as wise as you may, if you aren't wise, somewhere the pose becomes transparent; try to erase the tell-tale temper lines from your forehead; try to make eyes, weak from reading and study, lose their look of wistful wonder, their humility in the face of knowledge; try to make a greedy mouth generous, a mean mouth kind; try to make a lazy body as lean and vital as a dancer's; try to remove the look of dreamy meditation from a mystic's eyes. Oh! she thought, how truly in every sense we are what we are, and how truly do we give ourselves away!

And what am I? she asked herself ruefully, answering the question mercilessly: a poseur, a pretender, a vain little cheat! She, who had wept at Cyrano's "I carry my adornments on my soul. I do not dress up like a popinjay, but inwardly I keep my daintiness." That, she had decided when she had read it, was a thing to live by. And now see what she had done!

We'll fix that! she thought suddenly. Anything—humiliation, censure, public exposure—anything would be better than the punishment she was inflicting upon herself through shame! It was a wretched, miserable feeling, being ashamed, and she wouldn't go on with it another minute! It was senseless to go on. It was worse than useless. She tore the paper out of the machine, crushed it into a ball and threw it into the basket, closing her notebook and taking it with her.

In the center of town she parked her bike against an elm and walked swiftly to the door of the big yellow house next to the town office building. Her heart thumped frighteningly and she thought scornfully: Afraid! I'm a coward, too!

In response to her knock, a pleasant-faced lady came to the door.

"May I please speak to Mr. Hamilton?" Milly asked, hoping the lady might say that he had gone to Europe or to the dentist's or anywhere at all.

"Come in," the lady said. "I'll call him. He's in the garden. Gardening's his hobby, you know."

And so of course he'll just love to be interrupted by me! Milly thought dismally. Oh, dear!

He was frowning when he came in but his face lighted when he saw her. "Oh!" he said, "the report. Thought it might be you. Got it with you?"

Plunk! went her heart. "No," she said, "I—haven't."

His cold eyes searched her face ruthlessly. "What?" he demanded.

"It's not done. I don't know what you were talking about at the meeting. All I've got is a mess of stuff that doesn't make sense," she confessed hurriedly.

He looked at her as though she were a new species of insect. "Why didn't you say so?" he demanded irritably. "Why didn't you have gu— er, gumption enough to admit it was too much for you? We didn't have to hire someone from the school. We could have hired a professional stenographer. We only did it to give you young people a chance."

"I know," she said, studying her toes earnestly through the open spaces in her sandals. "I'm terribly sorry, Mr. Hamilton. I thought perhaps—"

"You thought what?" he snapped.

"That you'd tell me what it was all about," she plunged. "And I could go to the others and perhaps they'd repeat what they said. I know it's a lot of trouble to put you to but I'd like to make up in some way for—for not getting it."

He said something that probably was exactly what it sounded like: "Fool kid!" and walked to a window and looked out, scowling openly as he turned and faced her. "You couldn't possibly go to all the others," he said. "There were more than thirty there." Then, perhaps, moved in spite of his annoyance by her troubled face, he sighed and changed his tone. "But since there's only eight actually whose opinions amount to anything or whose statements we need to keep," he said decisively, "and since I'm one of those eight, guess we can work out something. Come on, sit down and I'll tell you what it was all about, since you don't know and we'll see if we can't make sense out of whatever you've got there. And next time, young lady, don't try to pass for what you aren't," he said incredibly.

She stared at him, stunned. Was he a mind reader?

She was not much surprised to learn that it had all been

about a new bridge. The town had been trying to buy land owned by Atherton Presby, who was holding out, demanding an outrageous price, knowing that the town—already in possession of the land on the opposite side of the river at that point, unable to secure another logical or suitable site for the bridge—had no choice but to pay what he asked. "Darned old pirate!" Mr. Hamilton grumbled. "He'll probably get away with it, too. Because we have to have it."

Listening intently as she read and hesitated and stopped, he managed to make astonishing sense out of her shreds and patches. In many places he was able to set her straight, not only on what he had said but on what the other men had said as well. Once or twice she saw him smiling at some of her blunders, but when he caught her eyes on him he instantly changed his expression and looked grimmer than ever. Finally he gave her the names of the seven other men whose opinions were important enough to keep and stressed that it would be absolutely necessary to check with each one to be sure that his remarks were authentic. He then wished her luck and said good-by with evident relief.

She scanned the list hastily and saw that Hamnet Hornsby's name was not on it. So it did not look as though she would have to confess her ignorance to the young man and his father! Some comfort, at least, she thought, for by this time she was certain that their names had been Hornsby. Curiously enough, the implications of the young man's statement that he stood beside his father and beside his father's property, failed to touch her at all.

She went to the drugstore and looked up the addresses of the men in the telephone book, finding happily that all but one lived pretty much in an area circling the center of town. Only Atherton Presby lived any considerable distance and since his house was on the outskirts of Ridge Road near Mayfair, she decided to save him till last. Elated by her first success, she started out hopefully. Glancing at her watch, she saw that it was close to eleven o'clock. With luck, she estimated, she might be able to go home for lunch and be done with her calls by one-thirty or two. Then she could go back to school and type the notes and still have the report done this afternoon!

She found five of the men at home before noon and was told that Mr. Pinwhitter would be in early in the afternoon. They were all tolerant, frequently amused, kind and willing in every case to help her. Her heart was light as she decided to skip lunch and finish the calling part of her task in one continuous performance.

She phoned her mother, then started pedaling out toward Mayfair, figuring she'd probably get there about one, humming as she skimmed along.

Nine Willoughby Road, Mr. Presby's house, was an old white colonial, its rambling lawn cut off from the road by a picket fence. She left her bike in the driveway and went confidently to the door, for this was the next to the last call, the only name left on the list except Mr. Pinwhitter's.

Her confidence died violently for, in response to the modest bang she gave the knocker, the red-haired young man came to the door! She had been mistaken! He was not Hamnet Hornsby's son but the son of Atherton Presby, the old pirate who was trying to take the town for all it was worth!

He was leaner, lankier than she had remembered, and even though his father was a pirate he had wonderful, clear blue eyes. Absorbing blue eyes that drew you in and really saw you and made it difficult, almost impossible for you to remember what you had been going to say.

"Uh— is, er— is Mr. Presby at home?"

His smiling mouth, she saw, was full and a little crooked, fascinating in its irregularity, and his teeth were white and glistening. She looked at him helplessly. "Junior or senior?" he grinned.

"Uh—senior."

"No, he isn't. But won't you come in, Miss Benton?

Perhaps I can help you. My name is the same as my father's but everyone I know calls me Ted."

He had remembered her name! Startling, incredible fact!

Flattered, shaken, she walked into a room that seemed to her big enough to build a house in. It was low-ceilinged, cool and peaceful; its book-lined walls splashed color. Even the dead ash in the grate looked friendly as though at any moment, wraith that it was, it would cease its silvery haunting and snap back to burning life. The only sound was the dry tick of an old wooden clock.

It seemed suddenly impossible to her that she should confess to Ted Presby that she was an absolute fake. Yet unhappily, sitting opposite him in the shadowy room, she braced herself for the effort: "I didn't get some of the things that were said at the meeting the other night," she admitted, opening her notebook, looking at it thoughtfully, seeing only his intent eyes bent upon her.

"My father and I have a habit of speaking very fast, especially when we're excited," he apologized. "It's no wonder you didn't get all of it. I'll be glad to help you if I can."

He evidently thought it was only what he and his father had said that she had failed to get!

Tempted. She felt herself tempted. The rest of the report now made fair sense and she could read it and when she came to his part or his father's he could simply fill in what they had said and need never know how stupid she was! He could go right on thinking that she hadn't gotten it all simply because he and his father had spoken too fast.

Yes, she could do that, couldn't she? Pass for what she was not?

No, oh no! Not if she had learned anything at all from her morning's experience.

"Well, I—I'm passing for what I am today," she blurted out hastily, "so I may as well admit that I didn't get much of the report at all. I went to Mr. Hamilton and told him and he straightened me out and gave me the names of seven other men to go to, so that I could make sense out of a completely senseless report. I've been to all of them now except Mr. Pinwhitter and your father. I didn't even have the names right," she said, a surprising feeling of confidence rising in her as she spoke the words that set her squarely where she belonged, honest, curiously unashamed.

Ted Presby laughed, a spark of admiration lighting in his eyes. "So you're passing for what you are today!" he said, looking at her with curious new interest. "There was a time, I remember, when Emerson hit *me*. Remember his 'Thou shalt read Homer, Aeschylus, Sophocles, Euripides, Plato, Proclus, Plotinus,' and so on?" He spoke slowly as though the taste of the words were sweet on his tongue, making them sound, through love, like music, touching her briefly by something she had never known before, something going past, through and beyond the moment.

"I seemed to see men as in a line," he continued, "each drawing from the one before and from all previous minds from the beginning of time till now. And I thought that it might be impossible for a man to pass for himself, to be original, to have thoughts of his own at all."

He was not talking to impress her, there was no question of that. He was simply thinking out loud. He was introducing her at once and without preliminaries to his true and inner self, a self that she felt sure everyone did not see. She smiled her silent acceptance and miraculously the confidence continued.

She was not exactly sure when they did begin to talk about the report, but finally they went over it and got it straightened out. There was, she found, a decided discrepancy between Mr. Hamilton's point of view and that of Ted Presby and his father. "We've been trying to *give* that land to the town for years," he explained, "but Mel Hamilton just wouldn't have it, said there was no use the town throwing away taxes on a useless hunk of mud. So when they finally decided they did want it, Dad thought it only fair to set a decent figure, the shoe being on the other foot, as it were."

Seeing him, she found it easy to see his father's point of view. But the wonderful thing, the thing she had not been prepared for, the thing she would always remember, was that when she had stepped into the room and begun talking to him, she had stepped out of her own particular orbit into another circle. Touching on its wider flow for the first time was like walking down a path in a dream, seeing vast shadowy trees, sentinel-still, seeing rolling meadows, purple hills in the heat of the sun on leaves and grass, making her glad to be there and alive, glimpsing fleetingly the elusive beauty of the soul.

She knew that at the moment the face and figure of Ted Presby lent enchantment to the experience. Yet if and when his figure faded, the vision would remain. It was a cool and lovely truth, there at the bottom of the wonderful moment, not to be confused with that moment, clear-headed, reasonable. She had taken a step forward—into something, out of something—and only by being herself!

An hour flew by like five minutes. Astonished, she saw that it was after two o'clock when she again picked up her bike, but in another world, another time than the one in which she had put it down.

She pedaled through a mist of springtime thinking: "Thou shalt read Homer, Aeschylus, Sophocles, Euripides . . ." The words repeated themselves, a magic chant in her mind: Homer, Aeschylus, Sophocles, Euripides . . . and he remembered my name! she thought. He remembered it!

As she pedaled over a rise in the road, it seemed to her that the sky had never been so blue before, the clouds so white, the sun so fierce and splendid.

Something
to Offer

SYLVIE SCHUMAN

Miss Carter's low-pitched voice carried through
the still classroom, back to where Viola Turner
sat, head on palm, dreaming out into the October
sky.

> How do I love thee? Let me count the ways.
> I love thee to the depth and breadth and height
> My soul can reach. . . .

The words struck into Viola like a rich minor chord,
starting sad music in her—at once sweet and bitter.

> I love thee freely, as men strive for Right;
> I love thee purely, as they turn from Praise.

How lucky Elizabeth Barrett was, despite her illness,
Viola thought. To have found someone who thought and

felt as she did. Would it ever happen to her? Faces of boys she'd known flew up out of the past, then blanked again. Boys she'd met through Kay. Faceless faces that had left no impress, as she had left none on them.

Her eyes veered toward Kay in the front row. Kay had always lived next door. They'd played stoop-ball as kids. But she couldn't call Kay her friend, despite the time they spent together talking about nothing. Kay was as empty as the boys she introduced her to. There was no real friend to share herself with.

> I love thee with a passion put to use
> In my old griefs. . . .

Did anyone here feel those words as she did? She looked around her. Most of the faces were glazed and bored or wore silly, embarrassed smiles. But in the second row Walter Davis leaned forward. Walter—a reporter on the school paper, nervously energetic, with a bite to his classroom comments. He was one of those she labeled "the interesting people." Amy Wright was another one. President of Student Council, witty, active in a dozen clubs. If only I could write or act or address a group, Viola thought, I might join them. But she had just herself to offer—her sincerity. She didn't fit in—not with Walter and Amy, not with Kay and her boy friends. . . .

The bell clanged and the class erupted into action. Miss Carter's voice was dinned out. But Viola still felt the mood of the sonnet, and now and then a phrase sang in her mind. She watched Kay picking invisible lint from Tom Enright's sleeve with red-tipped fingers. It was an unpleasant and familiar tableau.

Kay finally came over. "Sorry you waited, Vi. I won't be going home with you today. Tommy's taking me to lunch."

In a way, Viola was glad. "Well—then I'll run." She glanced at her watch, feigning concern over the time. "I have an auction to attend this afternoon." There was an expression in Tom Enright's eyes as he asked, "Auction?" which labeled her "queer."

She poured out of the building with a wave of other students. Like a little island in their midst stood Walter and Amy with two other couples, laughing and chatting on the stairs. They exuded an air of ease and belonging. She noted with a prod of jealousy Amy's arm linked through Walter's.

She turned up Fifth Avenue, with the Washington Square Arch looming in the distance. A crisp breeze tugged at her hair, and she tried not to think of Kay and Tom Enright—or Walter and Amy. Her mind darted ahead to the coming auction. There was that inkwell she wanted to bid on—wrought iron holding a crystal, clear and lovely as this fall day. It would go perfectly on her cherry desk. The thought conjured up the cluttered galleries, the faces of Pop Brown and Klirsky. Maybe she could not call them friends—she was more like a mascot to them. Still theirs were places where she was liked and felt free. . . .

The excitement of the auction was already dancing in her when she arrived home. The sun, streaming through the windows, lit the marble counter where her mother was making an ice cream soda. From the prescription booth came the clatter of her father's test tubes.

Viola laid a peck on her father's cheek, then went through the connecting door to their apartment in the back. She bolted down her meal, combed her straight auburn hair. Then she took some money from her desk drawer. She counted out a dollar and fifty-two cents with a pang of dismay. She was sure she'd saved more than that! In the store she asked her mother for fifty cents advance on her allowance.

Mrs. Turner's eyes were sharp. "Are you going to those auctions again?" She shook her head. "Honestly, I don't know what you see in them."

Her father put his head out from the prescription booth. "What do you expect from a girl raised on University Place? It's natural for her to hang around the auctions."

Mrs. Turner moved reluctantly to the cash register. "All right, but I still think it's a waste of time and money."

Viola was glad to get away. Her mother couldn't know what a joy it was to have a place where you were accepted, where you had friends, even if they were so much older.

She entered the bustle of Pop Brown's and was caught up in a host of familiar sights, sounds and smells. Inside the spacious rooms the air danced with dust motes. Pop was already barking, "I got five dollars, who'll make it six? Who'll make it six? Six, six, I got six. A fine old pewter dish, folks. Seven, I got seven. Going once for seven. Going twice for seven. Sold—for seven."

Viola squeezed into the crowd. There was her inkwell. If only her two dollars would buy it. . . . Her eyes scanned the crowd almost as professionally as Pop Brown's. She noted the dealers, the collectors, the rubberneckers who never bought anything, the bargain hunters and the ones like herself, who really loved the odd and singular pieces that showed up at auctions.

"Item twenty-five. Carved inkwell." Pop's eyes flicked toward hers. He knew she wanted it. "Fifty cents—who'll make it a dollar?" She raised her finger. "I got a dollar. One dollar I got."

"Dollar and a quarter!" someone cried.

Viola turned. The bid came from a dark man a few feet away. She looked at him sharply. A novice, she decided. "And a half," she said.

Pop tried to rush it. "Dollar and a half I got. Going once for a dollar and—"

"Two dollars," the man's voice rang out.

She hardly heard the rest of Pop's spiel. There was a lump in her throat. Pop gave her a chance. Then he banged the gavel. "Sold—to the gentleman for two dollars." Her inkwell. . . . There probably wasn't another one like it anywhere. Glumly she watched the rest of the bidding, one eye studying her rival. He was in his thirties, with thinning hair and brown eyes that moved constantly over the crowd. She couldn't place him in any of her categories. Pop was down to books now, and the crowd had dwindled. There was no one between herself and the stranger. Then, she found herself saying resentfully to him, "You didn't really want that inkwell, did you?"

His eyebrows went up. "Didn't I?"

"No. You bought it on the spur of the moment. I could tell from the way you bid." Disappointment made her bold. "I've had my eye on it since last week."

He took a step closer. "What do you mean—you could tell from my bidding? Is there a special way to bid other than just bidding?"

"Certainly. An experienced bidder never lets on that he's anxious. He just nods his head or raises a finger. The dealers don't even do that. They just motion with their eyes and Pop gets it."

"So I gave myself away." He studied Viola with interest. "Do you work here?"

"Oh, no. I live close by, and I've been coming here since I was ten. Not that I buy much—I don't have the money. That's why I was so disappointed about that ink-well—" She stopped short, suddenly aware of herself talking to a total stranger. "I'm sorry. It's not ethical to annoy someone who has outbid you." She started to walk away.

The stranger caught up with her. "Wait! You say you've been coming here since you were ten? Do you know every-one—the owner—?"

Something in his manner made her reply. "Not only here, but in Klirsky's Galleries down the block and the two across the street."

"Wonderful! Look," his voice held excitement, "maybe we can arrange a deal—"

"What kind of deal?"

"Well, it so happens you're right. I didn't want the ink-well. I bid just to get the feel of bidding. My name is Eric Taylor. I'm writing an article on auctions for a magazine and I'm collecting material. You could be a great help to me."

"But how can I be of use?" She eyed the inkwell long-ingly. He nudged it into her hand. It was good just to be holding it.

"We can start with Pop Brown. Any funny stories—peculiar traits? You know—human interest material," he asked.

"Well, yes. Pop's a sort of character. His real name is Oscar, which he hides. He started as a junkman and he's very proud of his success. He still has the cowbells that used to hang on his wagon. No matter how fine or expen-sive a piece is, Pop still calls it junk. Once when Jake was moving some rare china, Pop said, 'Hey, Jake! Watch out with that junk—it's precious.'"

Eric Taylor smiled and nodded. "Good—that's what I want."

She told Eric Taylor about Jake, the handyman who used to be a sailor and was studying engineering at night. She explained about inspection days and how you went about getting an appraisal, and about auction fever. "I've seen women pay a dollar for a cup worth only half that much," she said. "But when you start bidding, you get worked up. That's auction fever."

In the cluttered back office she introduced him to Mar-lene, the bookkeeper, who gave him some idea of an auc-tion's daily receipts. And she showed him one of Napoleon's desks that Pop refused to sell despite fabulous offers. The time passed. Eric Taylor looked at his watch. "I forgot. I've an appointment. You've been great, but we've only scratched the surface. Will you be here tomor-row?"

"Before I forget—" She took two dollars from her purse. "Thank you, very much."

He pushed it away. "Not at all. Thank *you*. You're a mine of information. A researcher's dream. I hope I can count on you for more."

He was actually giving her the inkwell! No, not really, for in a sense she had earned it. "I'll be here, Mr. Taylor," she promised.

"Good."

She left in an excited daze. Had this really happened? Eric Taylor. . . . She said the name over to herself. On a sudden impulse she headed toward the library.

She was awed to find him in *Who's Who.*

> Eric Taylor (1914–   ) Born, Gary, Indiana. Author of *Indiana Wind,* a novel, and numerous articles appearing regularly in national magazines. His most recent book, *Wild Blue Yonder,* recounts his experiences as Major in the Air Corps.

She found *Wild Blue Yonder* on the bookshelf and put in a reserve on the novel. She walked home studying the photograph on the book jacket, taken while in uniform.

Wonder filled Viola. Eric Taylor seemed so easy-going— not at all self-important. He was famous, and he wanted her to help him!

She couldn't wait for school to end the next day. She met Kay at the lockers. "Where you rushing to? I wanted to tell you about yesterday with Tommy. We went to a spaghetti joint—"

"Sorry, I've got a date." She noticed the surprised interest in Kay's eyes. "With a very important person," she couldn't resist adding.

Her spirits were high when she saw Eric. "Sorry I'm late." She had fussed with her outfit and taken extra pains with her make-up. She felt uneasy under his candid brown eyes. "There's Pop," she said hastily. "Want to grab him before the auction starts?"

"Whatever you say. Lead on."

"Hi, Pop," she greeted. "I want you to meet a friend of mine." She felt proud saying it. "Eric Taylor. He's writing an article on auctions."

Pop's eyes narrowed. "One of them muckrakin' fellows, huh? Well, I run an honest business, son. There's no up-bidding goes on here."

Eric said calmly, "You've got a wrong idea there, Mr. Brown."

"Of course. Mr. Taylor is very well known, Pop." Viola's tone was firm and chiding. "Why, people will come from everywhere to see this place when he writes it up."

Eric Taylor sent her a sidewise look. "I hear you have a desk of Napoleon's you refuse to sell, Pop. I think that shows real conviction."

Pop's face creased into a grin. "If Vi vouches for you, I guess you're all right. Besides, you have an honest face. An auctioneer gets to know faces."

As they entered the back office, Eric sent Viola a wink. Her heart did a somersault. Pop exhibited his desk with pride, answering Eric's questions. Before long, Pop began belaboring them with long-winded anecdotes—even dragging out a few that Viola hadn't heard before!

Back in the auction rooms, Viola pointed to a man in dark-rimmed glasses. "Collector," she whispered. "Glass. You know a piece is valuable if he starts bidding on it. The blonde is a dealer on Third Avenue. She buys only authentic pieces—mostly English. She'll bid high, because she sells high. She's a nuisance to someone like me. Now watch her bid. Just flicks her eyelashes and Pop gets the bid. She doesn't want it known what she buys—and for how much." A monstrous Victorian table was moved onto the dais. "Watch me call the bidders," Viola said with pride. "First, the fat lady in furs. She's obviously furnishing in Victorian—buys anything." A moment later the fat lady's finger jerked up. "Five dollars."

Viola beckoned toward an angular woman in black bangs. "Now she'll bid it up. She's a decorator. She'll trim off the gingerbread, refinish the table and sell it to a client at a fancy price."

"Seven," the decorator said.

"Where did you learn so much about antiques?" Eric asked.

"Oh, partly from the auctions. Partly from reading."

As the days went by, and then the weeks, she found herself talking a blue streak, pointing out things to Eric she'd never even realized she knew. They went from auction room to auction room, watching, listening, talking. But now only the Klirsky Gallery was left. Her mind fled from the fact that this must end soon. In her dreams it went on, with her becoming his assistant, traveling everywhere with him. "That's Eric Taylor's Girl Friday," people would point. Then someday. . . .

Stefan Klirsky had a mane of white hair and a lined face. His voice was cracked, yet musical, with the tinge of an accent. He said, "I have read your articles, Mr. Taylor, and I will tell you all I can."

As Klirsky lectured, Viola could see Eric responding just as she always did to the old man's feeling for fine things. They went to Klirsky's private office and he told them stories about famous pieces he'd sold, of phony antiques, reproductions and thefts. It was six o'clock when Klirsky stopped. Viola felt a pang. She could hardly make herself get out of the chair.

Eric was saying good-bye, shaking hands with Klirsky. Then they were standing outside. "Well, that about covers this area," Eric said. "I head for the uptown galleries next —Parke-Bernet . . ."

Her eyes went round. "The uptown galleries? I've always wondered about them, but—"

"You thought you didn't belong," Eric finished.

She was too choked to reply. He understood so well. How could she bear never seeing him again? She would drop back into her lonely world and Eric would become a dream.

She heard him saying, "Come on, for all this I at least owe you a dinner. Can you phone your folks?"

When she came out of the booth, Eric said, "We'll go to Dante's where the waiters sing opera."

The waiters were singing *Rigoletto* when they arrived. Eric lit a cigarette and ordered wine. He handed her the menu. She felt very grownup and her cheeks were warm with excitement.

Eric raised his glass to her. "A toast to Violet—delicate and shy."

She flushed and couldn't meet his eyes. "I hate that about being shy."

"I know. I used to hate being shy, too."

"You?" Her brows arched in surprise. "You're hardly shy."

"I used to be. Painfully, agonizingly shy. When I was younger. I couldn't look at a girl. I was awkward. I was lonely."

"It doesn't seem possible," she said. "You're so at ease. So—" She deliberated on a word and picked "urbane."

He smiled a little at the choice. "A long time has gone by since then. I've traveled, met people, worked hard—achieved a little. You will, too."

She couldn't hold it back any longer. In her whole life he was the one person who'd ever been so honest. Tears brimmed to her eyes. "But you're a writer," she said, "and I'm nothing. I don't fit anywhere."

"Nonsense. You're a pretty little lady with a good head on her shoulders. And you've been a great help to me."

His emphatic tone made her smile. She blinked away her tears.

"And someday," he went on, toying with his glass, "you're going to be a great help to yourself. Now let's have our coffee."

She wished the evening would never end. But at eight o'clock Eric said, "Your family will think I kidnaped you." He walked her home. She introduced him to her parents and then stood outside with him as he waited for a taxi. This was really the end. She tried to stretch it out by mentioning the uptown galleries. There was a silence. Finally Eric said, "Why don't you come along? Here's your opportunity to see them."

She had a feeling she'd forced him into it. A taxi pulled over. "Ten o'clock, Saturday, Parke-Bernet. I'll meet you."

Saturday was a rare fall day, offering the last warmth of sun. Viola took the Fifth Avenue bus uptown. She got off a few blocks before her stop. She was early and peeked into the shop windows. She caught her reflection in them—her figure trim in green corduroy, a matching cloche highlighting her reddish hair. She wanted to look her best.

Suddenly she saw Eric waiting near the Parke-Bernet building. She started to rush forward when she noticed someone with him. A girl. A tall, striking girl in black. The girl followed his gaze and smiled. Viola made herself smile back.

"Here she is," Eric said, "my wonderful assistant." It sounded to Viola as though they'd been discussing her. The girl's name was Nelia Robinson. "My fiancée," Eric added.

Past the constriction in her throat she was saying, "I'm delighted to meet you, Miss Robinson."

As they stepped into the large marble lobby, everything ran together in a mass of color and movement—the elevator taking them upstairs, the quiet, heavily rugged room into which they moved, the scent of perfumes and the delightful musty odor of antiques. Lining the walls was a clock collection, chiming now and then with distant music.

"Isn't this a beautiful clock, Viola?" Nelia started to look in the catalogue for a description of it.

"It's Queen Anne," Viola told her. "You can see by the inlay."

"You're right," Nelia said. "That's just what the catalogue says—'Queen Anne, excellent example of Dutch marquetry.'"

Eric was talking to a tall, distinguished man, bringing him over. "I want you to meet Viola Turner. You know Nelia, of course. Viola, this is John Macy."

John Macy—the famous playwright!

"John is an old antique hound," Eric said. They started in a group to the auction room and Viola realized with a wonder that deepened her distress that these friends of Eric's accepted her as though she were someone. She sat between Eric and Nelia. During a lull in the bidding, Nelia asked, "Are you planning to be a decorator?"

"I hadn't thought of it."

"Of course, if you're as thorough and discerning as Eric says, there are any number of things you might do well—research, for instance."

"She has an eye like a hawk," Eric put in. "She could be a detective—or a photographer. Incidentally, Nelia is a photographer."

They wanted her to lunch with them, but she made excuses. "I promised mother I'd get back early." There was an awkward silence. Then Nelia said, "Oh, there's Jane Michales. I must see her a moment." She turned to Viola. "I'm so glad I met you."

She and Eric were alone. She was sure Nelia had arranged it. "Well, which do you prefer—Parke-Bernet or Klirsky?"

"Klirsky." A lump rose in her throat at the memory of their day there. "Eric. . . . Well, I guess it's good-bye."

Eric took her hand. "Good-bye, Viola. Thank you again. I'll send you a card from South America." Her eyes were questioning. "I'm doing a piece on the coffee industry next. I'll have to learn Spanish, among other things."

She looked at him as though trying to photograph him in her memory. She knew she should leave now. "South America? That's so far away. . . . Are you going alone?"

He nodded. "Alone—into a strange land where I don't know a soul. It'll be an adventure."

She said, "Good-bye, Eric." Then she turned and walked swiftly to the elevator.

At school she was like an automaton. The days blew by like the last dead leaves, aimless and barren. Kay was distant—estranged by the three weeks in which Viola was taken up with Eric. They smiled politely to each other in class. Viola noticed that she had attached herself to a new boy.

Evenings were worst. She was tired of reading and listening to music. She took long walks, stopping sometimes outside the neighborhood "Y." She'd scan the posters of the cultural activities with blurred longing and walk on.

"You're losing weight," her mother observed. "I'm going to ask your father for a tonic."

She didn't need medicine. She needed someone to talk to. "I'm all right. I just feel—blue."

Her mother's eyes held their own thoughts. "Naturally, when you're run down you get that way."

Viola sat at her desk and stared at the feathery snow drifting down—the first snow of the season. It coated the limbs of an ailanthus tree and threw a pearly light into her room, filling her with dreams and discontent. She wondered where Eric was now. She tried to imagine South America, but could only call up some tangled jungle or an unreal technicolor movie set. She thought back to Dante's and dining with Eric. Despair burrowed in her.

The phone was ringing in the store and then she heard her father calling her. She lifted the annex phone in their apartment and Kay's voice came over, bright and metallic.

"Look, a friend of mine just came to town. He wants to make a foursome. I understand this Roger is a dream boat. I'm almost tempted myself." Kay put in an appeasing chuckle. "What d'you say, Vi? It'll be like old times."

She was aware that her palms were damp. She hadn't had a date in a long time. It might take her mind off Eric. One part of her said "Go" while another thought "What for?" She couldn't make herself answer in this state. "I'll call you back," she said, "in ten minutes."

She remained at the telephone table. It was five-thirty. Snowy twilight, with lights going on over the city. Everywhere girls were getting ready to go out. Eager, contented girls. Worrying only about the fit of their dresses, the proper curl to their hair. They'd go out and have fun.

She could anticipate the evening—the appraisal on meeting, the hope rising. The boy would like her at first. Boys usually did. Yes, it would start off fine, but then. . . . She thought of Kay's description of Roger. Baseball hero. Every girl's dream. A de luxe edition of the types she had met through Kay in the past. The evening would wear on with Roger discoursing of batting averages and the standing of the Major League teams until she became dull and glassy-eyed. She'd begin to feel there was something wrong with her . . . and Kay would be riding high.

She dialed Kay's number. "I'm sorry . . . a previous appointment . . . thanks. . . ."

She slept poorly and was late reporting to her first class. She noticed a slight stir as she stepped through the door. I must be imagining things, she thought, taking her seat. She saw Kay's head twisting around, and here and there other students turned to look at her. She grew self-conscious. Maybe her slip was showing or there was a smudge on her face. She took out her compact. No, everything was in order. She was grateful when Miss Carter got the session under way.

A neighbor pressed something into her hand. It was a

note. "Like to see you after class. Please wait. Walter Davis."

Walter's quick blue eyes were scanning her face and he was smiling. "Say—you've been hiding your light under a bushel. We didn't know you were an expert on auctions and antiques."

"How—how did you find out?"

"Don't tell me you haven't seen the magazine article on auctions with that plug, 'Petite, russet-haired Viola Turner,'" he quoted. "That's you—or isn't it?"

She stared in disbelief. The article! She'd almost forgotten about it. Eric had something about her in it. What? A hundred questions bubbled in her. Was that why the class had noticed her this morning?

"Look, I want a write-up on you for the school paper," Walter was saying. "How about lunch tomorrow? You can tell me the story of your life then."

"All right—tomorrow." Then she was plunging downstairs, her mind eddying with anticipation. She, in a national magazine! Curiosity consumed her, made her take the steps two at a time.

She bought a copy and started reading as she walked back to the school building. Her eyes devoured the pages. There it all was—Pop Brown and Klirsky and the fat woman who bought Victorian—all vividly organized into a pattern of information and entertainment. And suddenly, thrillingly, her name leaped out at her.

Russet-haired, petite Viola Turner can be seen at most downtown auctions, brightening the dingy rooms. Deceptively dreamy in appearance, she has a shrewd eye for character and a bargain. The small amounts of money she spends here bring her good value and entertainment equal to a Broadway show. This bright teen-ager, a sort of mascot around the auctions, is an example of how 'auction fever' infects young and old.

She couldn't wait to show it to her parents. She burst into the store. "Mom, Pop—look!"

Her father's eyes kindled. "Well, well, my daughter's name in print." He laid aside some capsules, studied the page.

"What do you know!" Her mother's voice held amazement. "Maybe those antiques weren't a waste after all." She measured Viola with a new respect. "Give me that magazine. I want to show Mrs. Corcoran next door."

Viola laughed as her mother hurried out. She felt suddenly strong and alive. Outside the sun was brilliant, glinting upon snowy roof-tops. She wrapped a woolen scarf around her head and went out, walking along with head high, taking firm strides against the bracing air.

She had something to offer—she had had it all along. Perhaps it wasn't important—although Eric and Nelia and even John Macy had respected her small knowledge—but it didn't have to be important. If not for her interest in auctions, she would never have met Eric. And none of this would have happened. A person, in a way, totaled up to his interests. Walter with his newspaper work and Amy with her organizational activities. And Kay . . . she had no interests outside herself—her conquests of boys. It was the reason she'd found Kay wanting. She remembered her awe of the uptown galleries, only to find her knowledge stood her in good stead there, too.

She paused at the "Y" and a familiar name leaped from the bulletins. "Tonight: John Macy lecturing on The Current Theatre." John Macy! She had met him! She would go to hear him. Why not? She looked over the other posters, describing courses. "Theatre Workshop." "Photography." "Interior Decorating." She heard Nelia Robinson's voice again: "Are you planning to become a decorator?" She would take the course, she decided.

She went up the front steps, her heart pounding with excitement. There seemed so many things to do all of a sudden. At the top step she paused, the memory of Eric Taylor whelming in her. His words came back: "Someday you're going to be a great help to yourself." The meaning lit in her mind.

She went into the "Y." She would ask about the course, register perhaps. Tonight she would attend John Macy's lecture. And tomorrow she had a lunch date with Walter Davis. It was a new and beckoning world.

After the Ball

SAMSON RAPHAELSON

BEACHTOWN, Long Island. Midnight in June. Music in the air. A girl, hidden in black shadow behind a high hedge, peered through the hedge across tops of cars in a parking lot, watching the two great rear windows of the high school beyond, feasting on the sight of couples dancing at the Senior Ball. She was a slender girl, sixteen, not tall and not small, with oversize eyes and mouth in a delicate, piquant face. She wore a thin cotton jumper dress and, over her shoulders, a light cardigan sweater. Her thick brown hair was moist from sea spray; her unusually long, strong, beautiful hands clutched a pair of flat-heeled shoes with socks stuffed in them; and her bare feet on the dewy grass were still crusted with sand from the beach nearby. The girl's name was Mady Schiffen. She was, perhaps, the most promising young pianist in the world, and several hours ago she had run away from home.

It was after dinner, about seven, in the small brownstone

house west of Central Park, and she had just finished helping her mother with the dishes. Rudolf Schiffen was lingering over his coffee, studying the music sheets of Beethoven's Sonata No. 23 in F Minor, Opus 57, otherwise known as the *Appassionata*. He was a thin, bald, fiercely artistic-looking man, a Vienna-born piano teacher and the son of a piano teacher. Mady came into the dining room and said, in her correct, slightly accented English, "Excuse me, pa-pa. I'd like to go out to the drugstore, please, for some tooth paste."

"Tooth paste?" Her father looked blankly over his spectacles. Then, with an air of patience more terrifying than the furies he thought he was concealing, he said, "May I ask, how can tooth paste come into your head at a time like this? I inquire only out of curiosity."

"Well, pa-pa, I—"

"Do you know what day is today?"

"Yes, pa-pa, Friday."

"And tomorrow—you know what is tomorrow, twenty-four hours from now or—let us be exact—twenty-six?"

"Yes, pa-pa. Carnegie Hall."

"And what will you be doing in Carnegie Hall?"

"Playing the piano, pa-pa."

"Good. Very good. Now may I ask: Do you use your teeth in playing the piano?"

"No, pa-pa."

"What do you use, by the way?"

"My—my hands, pa-pa."

"Wrong. You know that is wrong, don't you? Your hands?"

Mrs. Schiffen appeared in the kitchen doorway. She was a plump, pink-cheeked *Hausfrau*.

She said mildly, "Let her go to the drugstore. It has been such a hot day and—"

"Your hands!" Mr. Schiffen ignored Mrs. Schiffen. With even greater patience, he said, "Do you deliberately say such a thing to insult my intelligence?" Mady, of course, knew it was more than hands, but she had thought, after tooth paste and teeth, that he had wanted a literal answer. She also knew that any explanation would make things worse, so she said nothing. "Haven't I told you a thousand times," Mr. Schiffen went on, "that it is your heart, your soul, your mind? Your musical intelligence—you had it once, if only a little—that's what you use at the piano. Feeling, form, insight, imagination. Not tooth paste."

Mrs. Schiffen had gone back humbly and serenely into the kitchen, which was how it always had been.

Mady said, "Yes, pa-pa. I just want to go for a few minutes to the corner and—"

"Go," Mr. Schiffen said. "But on your way contemplate, for example, this F Minor Sonata. Ask yourself, 'Are my hands making only loudness when my soul should be making a storm? Will I fool anybody with quick fingers if my brain is elsewhere? Does tenderness come from soft notes and a slow tempo, or from the heart?'"

"Yes, pa-pa."

"And on the way back, remind yourself that tomorrow night, on that platform, there will be no hands at all. Only you—you and a piano, not separate, but together—one. And not alone. Beethoven will be there, too; and Mozart, and Schubert, and Schumann. And all the rest is an audience. It has been waiting for you a year—ever since we stepped off the boat. Your first American audience, hungry, thirsty. The most demanding audience in the world, but the most grateful. For music, not tooth paste."

"Yes, pa-pa," Mady said. Then she went into her room, shut the door and stood very still.

It was not the first time she had thought of running away. She had thought of it hundreds of little times and nine big times. The nine big times happened before each of her nine big recitals. Always, a few days before the recital— even that first one, in Zurich, when she was five years old

—she had been all but possessed by a wildly desperate impulse to open the door, walk out and disappear. The little times happened in between. Maybe on a day when she was unusually tired after practicing the regular nine hours. Or a day when pa-pa was in bad humor, and she would be reminded bitterly that he was never satisfied with her playing, that he had dismissed all the glowing things the newspapers had said about her in important cities like Vienna and Paris and London, that he had never once shouted, "Bravo!" Or an evening when she would be sitting with a tutor—one of the many middle-aged females who flowed through her life so that she could have history and languages and mathematics without going to school. Or a Sunday when, after church, she and pa-pa and ma-ma took their weekly walk in a park, boys and girls shouting and jostling around them.

As I say, it was not the first time. In fact, she had had it in mind all week, ever since the heat wave began and she had read the advertisement about Beachtown in the Travel and Resorts section of last Sunday's paper. And now she did it. She pulled the small canvas bag down from the high closet shelf and packed it quickly, having long known that she would take almost nothing with her and would make her plans as she went along and be magnificently unsystematic and free for the rest of her life. She checked the money in her purse—a few dollars in change. From underneath a stack of tattered music sheets on the closet floor she took an envelope containing fifty dollars in bills, her lifetime savings.

Then she remembered the ad. She found it in the drawer of her table. Under a lovely picture of a beach with handsome girls and men romping in the surf, it said:

WHY SWELTER IN TOWN? BE 15 GUARANTEED DEGREES COOLER—ONLY 2 HOURS AWAY! COME AND MEET FRIENDLY PEOPLE IN THE FRIENDLY OCEAN AT FRIENDLY OCEAN MOTEL IN BEACHTOWN, LONG ISLAND!

She stuffed the ad into her purse. Bag in hand, she slipped out of the apartment and kept going until nine-thirty, when the train stopped at Beachtown.

She arrived at the Friendly Ocean Motel, where it was blessedly cool, just as the ad had promised. She tipped the taxi driver a dollar, registered as "Mary Schmidt, New York"; then tipped the puzzled motel manager two dollars, saying, "You need not accompany me, please. The bag is light, thank you." She stayed in her room just long enough to take the money from her purse, and a handkerchief, and button them into a pocket of her jumper dress. Then, in no time at all, she was on the long, wide, empty beach, cardigan over her shoulders, shoes and socks in her hand, scudding bare-legged into and out of surf foaming white under a three-quarter moon, the sea wind beating against her scant clothes, utterly alone with the beauty and terror of her freedom, going on and on until she heard the dance music from afar, above the dunes.

And now she was behind the high hedge, spellbound, watching the couples beyond the two big open windows— the boys in their rented white coats, the girls filmy in pastel colors—memorizing every tune and harmony of the rock-and-roll numbers and the slow fox trots and waltzes, every chance remark caught by the night air; preserving in her mind forever the last hour of the Senior Ball of Beachtown High.

Too soon the orchestra was playing *Good Night, Sweetheart*. It was not a good orchestra, there was very little talent in any of the four pieces, but Mady, who ordinarily would have shuddered at mediocrity, was loving it all, and there were tears in her eyes when it was over. Sad and insatiable, she watched the two streams of girls and boys— one coming out the back door set between the windows, the other down the sloping alley from the front. They were no longer deadpan, as in the dance ritual, but laughing and humming and calling to one another. Car doors slammed, motors coughed and snorted, headlights blazed, backed and disappeared.

With a flick, the arcs over the deserted parking lot blinked out, and with another flick the two great windows went dark, and now Mady, feeling the cold in her bare feet, put on her socks and shoes, but there was nowhere she wanted to go. Next thing she knew, she was trying the knob of the back door. It was open, and there she was in the school gym, its character barely visible in the windowed moonlight. The grand piano was so near that she almost fell over it.

She paused at the piano, a hand resting on the keys, while she looked around in the silver-and-black darkness at the balcony that lined the three other walls, at the streamers, the painted panels, the Chinese lanterns. She sat down, hungry to relieve every tune and harmony and rhythm she had heard, to play the evening over again for herself. She skimmed the keys. The piano was in tune, and she liked its tone, even with the top down. Then she worked into the keyboard softly with her stiff, cold fingers, doing all sorts of movements from one end of the piano to the other so that her wrists would become flexible and her finger tips alive, and she wasn't aware of the boy coming in through the back door until his white jacket loomed up beside her.

"Don't stop," he said quickly, before she could get frightened. "Gosh, you certainly can tickle those ivories." He moved over to the curve in the piano, and she could see him better, a tall boy with a large, open, guileless face. "What you playing?"

"Oh, I am only warming my fingers. Just going up and down."

"Sounds real tricky, no kidding."

She saw that it was a compliment and smiled at him and said, "Thank you," looking with interest at the first boy in her new life.

He said, "I dropped in to search for an earring. I have a flash and all." He showed the flashlight in his hand. "It belongs to my girl friend. I mean the earring. She lost it while dancing or something. Maybe sitting down. She had two, but she lost one. I mean I don't want you to think I'm a night prowler or one of those unbalanced maniacs you read about."

"Oh, I don't!" Mady assured him. "And *I* am not also."

The boy stared at her, then smiled. "That's a pretty humorous remark," he said. Then gaining assurance, he said, "I take it for granted you're here for the weekend or something along that line."

"Yes, you are right."

"I'll make a guess that you came with at least one parent or maybe a married sister."

"Oh, you are a good guesser!" Mady said with real gratitude. "And we are not long in America. My sister's husband, he is a steamship captain, and I travel with them because I am an orphan. So tonight, when my sister and husband were in the motel asleep, I took a walk and listened outside to your dance. I liked so much the music, and I have a good memory, so I came in and—"

"Can you play *I'm Gonna Sit Right Down*? It goes like this."

He started humming, and she interrupted after the first phrase, "Oh, yes!"

"Let's hear it."

"But the earring of your girl friend—she must be waiting."

"Not her," the boy said, rolling the flashlight along the floor until it hit the wall. "She's asleep in bed by now. All she wants to know is I'm here looking for it. I mean, you're sitting in a car saying good night after an affair like the Senior Ball, what's an hour more or less? Nobody's going to sneak over and steal that earring. I mean, it's no rajah's priceless gem, believe me. But that's the type she is. She's shallow, on my word of honor."

"Oh," Mady said, fascinated. "You had a quarrel?"

"Want to know the truth? It was mutual. I mean it's beyond earrings. Our relationship is at the boring stage."

"Relationship—what is that?"

"Say, how old are you, anyway?"

"Sixteen."

"Well, you ought to know. I mean you're either going steady or it's nothing. Well, if you're going steady, pretty soon it becomes a relationship. I mean you get acquainted, and then there's nothing to talk about, is what I mean. I'm probably pretty shallow myself. Seventeen years and nothing to show for it except a lousy high school diploma— if I get it."

"What is your name?"

"Vernon. What's yours?"

"Mary."

"You going to play, Mary?"

"Oh, yes! Yes—Vernon!"

She gave him a quick smile; then bent over the piano, hands poised lovingly. Her cardigan slipped from her shoulders to the floor, and he came around, picked it up, and sat beside her on the bench. He watched as her long fingers stroked the keys, feeling their way into the piece, first the drumming bass chords for rhythm, then a brilliantly accurate evocation of the melody, and then the jolting rambunctious totality that she made of *I'm Gonna Sit Right Down and Write Myself a Letter*. Without looking, she felt his swaying, entranced response, and she gave back tenfold, making new forays on the tune, possessing and repossessing it, tantalizing its rhythms without betraying the beat; and again she didn't hear the door open, nor did she know that the boy Vernon had gone until he slid back on the bench and, out of the shadows, dancing, came two white coats and two fluffy dresses.

Her hands faltered, but did not stop, and the two couples, now dancing beside the piano, didn't miss a step as Vernon named their names, Jane and Audrey and Bill and Stan.

He said in a very respectful manner, "They were passing by and they heard the music. So I told them about you and the captain of the steamship and all. I mean, they wanted to dance, and I said I didn't think you'd mind."

Mind? She answered by rocking and rolling them into another remembered tune, and now, following them with her eyes, she outdid herself, converting every shading of seen pattern into its musical counterpart—each sway and swerve and pivot and tilt, and the Spanish-gypsy-like elegance of the crackling, snapping pauses.

When she finished, the filmy dresses and the white coats rushed to her and gave tribute. How lucky they were, the girls babbled; they had been in Stan's car, looking at the sea, and they were just on their way to the jukebox café for another hour of dancing, but this had it over any jukebox. Honestly, said the girls; no kidding. And the boys muttered fervent agreement, saying it was the coolest and the most, and that *they'd* say. And the girls asked eagerly if she would play some more.

"Oh, yes!" Mady said. "I will play all night, if you want."

The boys said how's for a slow fox trot, and Mady, about to bend again over the piano, glanced at Vernon, who had not moved or uttered a word. His face was in the shadow, and she twisted her head to see his expression.

She said softly, "And you, Vernon—did you like the music, yes?"

He turned slowly and looked at her. He tried twice to talk and failed. Then he said, "I—" Then he said, "Uh-huh." Then he looked away.

A boy was in love with her!

Her hands fell on the keyboard, breaking into gaily

romantic clusters of chords, and she wove drolleries into
the slow fox trot, for she was simmering with laughter at
the beautifully ridiculous idea that somebody loved her.
The smitten boy himself was forgotten, a blur at her
side, while she sailed on into a waltz, laced it with lan-
guishing naughtiness and then mocked it with dissonate
outbursts, as a young girl on a hayride, embraced, might
break into an arpeggio of giggles from sheer intolerable
bliss. Then, with more rock-and-roll, more of every number
she had heard that evening, throwing in a few other numbers that came to her from the nowhere, perhaps from a
radio in some unknown neighbor's apartment, she kept
soaring on the wings of her uproariously comic idea.

She was only dimly aware of other things going on. The
night watchman, for instance, who appeared suddenly in
the far front door, brandishing a flashlight, and as suddenly disappeared, immobilized by Stan, who probably
bribed him. And the five more couples. They had reveled
in the jukebox place until it closed, and on their way home
they, like the first two couples, had been halted by the un-
wonted sounds emerging from the dark high school building. Somebody—not the love-anchored Vernon this time—
must have explained, and welcomed them to join the party,
for there they were, making it seven white coats and seven
filmy dresses on the floor.

And now it was over, for Mady came in orderly memory
to the last tune she had heard. *Good Night, Sweetheart.*
Without knowing the title or the words, she knew its meaning, and she played it first lyrically, with the sadness of
farewell, and then, because of the laughter in her, she
whipped into it again with a thumping, stamping beat,
shredding it with scurrilous harmonies, finishing high, wild
and handsome.

They swarmed upon her. Vernon muttered introductions.
They told her, no kidding, that it was out of this world, and
gosh, a girl asked her, where did she learn to play like that?

And a boy said not to be corny, that that stuff is born in you. And another girl said she bet that any one of the big resorts would be glad to give Mary a job playing dinner dances, and another boy, asking the girl how dumb could she get, offered to bet that Mary already had made records with some big-name band. And then they were asking where she was staying and for how long and what was her last name, and could she play classical as smooth as she played pop, but before Mady could think of an answer, somebody else said gee, would they look at the length of those hands, and it zigzagged like that until a girl cried, "What do you know—it's after three!"

Mady watched with moist eyes as the last white coat and the last filmy dress disappeared and the door swung shut after them. Then she turned to Vernon, and there, on a piano bench alongside a piano, occurred her first kiss. The moon, lower now, beamed in horizontally; she could see Vernon's face; his tightly closed eyes gave him a reverent expression which revived the hilarity in her. Not daring to laugh, she broke gently from his embrace.

"Those noisy cars," she said, jumping up. "Let us see them as they go, one by one. And then, if you like, I play some more—only for you, yes?"

She picked up her cardigan and darted to the window just in time to wave at the first car as it swung out. Then Vernon came up and, without a word, drew her from the window into the shadows. This time she, too, shut her eyes. The preposterousness was gone. This, not the other, was her first kiss. It was Chopin.

When finally she stirred out of his arms, there were no sounds from the parking lot, and Mady, back at the window, cried, "All gone! Only one empty car is left." Vernon had joined her and was staring broodingly at the ivory-and-chrome convertible with its top down, which stood gleamingly alone in the parking lot. "It is yours, yes?"

Vernon said, "It's brand new. Do you like it?"

"Oh, yes. It is so chic!"

"There's only a hundred and fifty miles on it. It was just delivered this afternoon. I mean it's my graduation present." He took her in his arms and said, still broodingly, "Look—all kidding aside—do you really like the car?"

"How could anybody not like it?"

"O.K. Because I've got an idea. Quite an idea."

"Yes, Vernon?"

"First I want to ask you—" He paused, overcome by the earnestly listening face, and he kissed her a few more times, long enough for the declining moon to fall beyond and below the window, changing the silver light in the gym to gray and the gray shadows to black.

"Now," he said, after the kiss, "regarding this idea that crossed my mind."

"Yes, dear Vernon?"

"Well, first I want to know— Look, let's be adult about this. I mean kissing is one thing, and liking a person is a different department, if we have to be frank. So what I want to know—and strictly on the level, *entre nous*—I mean don't be afraid of hurting my feelings, because I'm rugged. What I want to know is: Do you honestly like me as much as I like you? That's all. It's that simple."

"Well, it is not—that is not a simple question, Vernon. You—"

"Skip it. I'm serious. I want a yes or a no."

"Why—yes. Of course! Oh, yes, I do!"

"Fine. O.K. Now you've already stated that you like the car. Correct?"

"Correct."

"So far, so good. I take it for granted that you know about the first thousand miles, of course. I mean a new car isn't broken in until that old speedometer says one thousand. That's true in Europe, Africa, anywhere anybody comes from. Right?"

"Er—right!"

"And there's nothing sweeter than that first thousand miles, handling a beautiful thing like that—I mean everything has to be done just so. You can imagine it all, can't you?"

"Yes, yes!"

"O.K. Now we come to the idea which occurred to me. The way I get it, girls in the old country marry pretty young. I mean I take that for granted. So I was thinking, suppose you and I keep on getting acquainted along the same line as now. After all, if two persons have a lot in common, it shouldn't take forever, should it?"

"N-no."

"O.K. Comes the dawn, as they say. We have breakfast overlooking the beach at Gurney Inn; then we drop around at the motel, I meet your sister and her husband, and we talk things over. I mean I'm not just a flash-in-the-pan, fly-by-night proposition. My father is pretty highly regarded in the building and contracting business, and—as for my family's angle, that's in the bag. I mean, Dad is a college graduate himself, and my mother was a nurse; they're real modern in their psychology. I mean, anything I want, they're favorably inclined. So—it occurred to me it would be mighty neat, you and I in the car, putting on that eight hundred and fifty miles in the shape and form of a honeymoon. Do you follow my trend?"

"I—I think so."

"I'm just mentioning it as a thought that crossed my mind, that's all."

Mady's eyes, brilliant with excitement, were studying him, measuring him. She said, "It is a very interesting thought."

"Don't take it seriously unless you feel like it."

"Oh, I feel like it," she said, with intensity.

"You do?"

"Oh, yes!"

"You mean—now don't confirm this unless you're sure—

but if you're saying something along the line that you love me—"

"Oh, yes, I love you, Vernon. I am feeling much more than love for you."

"You are?"

"I feel—" He put his arms around her. "I feel so much. If I could only—" She rested her head against his chest, eyes closed. "If I could only play it for you!"

"Oh, you don't have to," Vernon said quickly.

She looked up. "Do you know the first movement of Beethoven's *Appassionata?*"

"Can't say that I do."

"That is how I feel! And the second movement—it is even more how I feel!" She was out of his arms. "I think maybe—yes, I shall play it. Would you like?"

"Well—aren't you tired?"

"Tired? Me? Tonight?"

The moon had set, but the early dawn of June, rising on the front side of the school, was reflected from the sky, and Mady could distinguish the two ends of the keyboard, which was enough. Vernon, sitting on the window sill, scarcely heard the Beethoven piece. The gaiety and depth, the sheer musical excitement of the *Appassionata* was for him background music as he gazed out at his convertible and dreamed ineffable dreams.

However, before Mady had completed the first movement, there were others to listen. They came on tiptoe through the front doors high at the far end of the balcony—the night watchman, followed by Mr. and Mrs. Schiffen, followed by the motel manager, and two Beachtown policemen, and several New York reporters and a photographer. They stopped on the balcony, and when Mr. Schiffen had listened a minute or two, he made violent gestures commanding everybody to sit and to be absolutely still. The gestures were unnecessary, for everybody had been still and remained very still until, after the third movement's tumult, came the final abrupt flourish of the end. Then their handclapping sputtered from the balcony, and Mady, startled, looked around just in time to see her father clambering over the rail.

He was coming toward her, arms outstretched, crying, "Bravo!"

She rose from the piano bench, trembling. "Bravo!" he cried again, and she realized that it was indeed her father and that he truly was saying "Bravo!" to her, about herself. He kept coming, and a third time, louder, he shouted "Bra-vo!" Mady sobbed and ran to meet him.

As she flung herself into his arms, the photographer, who had raced for position, caught it with a blue-white streak of strobe. The next minute Mady was embracing her mother, and the photographer shot that too. Then the lights went on in the gym, and pictures were being taken of everybody; and the reporters were asking the dazed Vernon all sorts of questions; and the motel manager, proudly swinging Mady's canvas bag in his hand, told again and again how he had had a hunch and notified the police, but on the other hand, shucks, it was all in a day's work.

After a while it was over, and everybody was hustling up the stairs toward the front entrance—that is, everybody but Vernon. Mady, exhausted now, clinging to her mother and father, was still answering questions when they reached the sidewalk in the dawn. They took a last picture of Mady in the front seat of the hired car. Mr. Schiffen at the wheel and Mrs. Schiffen smiling from the back seat. Then one of them said, "How would you like to stay here?"

"Here?"

"And be a high school girl, go to dances, have dates like other boys and girls?"

"You mean live here all the time, with those—" She was about to say, "those *children?*" but she stopped herself out of politeness. Then she suddenly sat up.

"Vernon!" she cried.

"I think he went out the back way," the reporter said.

She flung open the door of the car, and nobody followed her as she raced to the sloping side alley and back down toward the parking place. The empty convertible was still there, long and low, reflecting the pink sky in its ivory surfaces. She rushed to the open back door and into the gym. The lights had been turned off again, and for a moment she saw no one in the luminous gray. Then, moving toward her on the floor in the balcony's shadow, came the small pale circle of a flashlight.

"Vernon?"

The circle stopped and went dark, and she could see the white coat behind it. It was Vernon.

He mumbled, "I came back to look for that earring."

"Oh." Mady moved a step toward him. "I will help you!"

"Skip it. I'll buy her another pair." Suddenly he was going past her to the rear door, saying over his shoulder, "So long."

She caught up with him and walked beside him in silence to the convertible. She stood by as he got into it and started the motor. Then she reached to him, and he took his hands off the wheel and held her as closely as he could against the door's thickness, and she kissed him, delicately, with wisdom and tenderness.

"So long, Vernon!"

She started to go; then paused and caressed the proud, swelling sweep of the front fender. "It is the most beautiful car in the world," she said.

She stepped back as Vernon, looking straight ahead, set the car in gear and moved away. She watched its gleaming perfection curving around last night's hedge into a side road, watched until its whiteness disappeared over the top of a hill, leaving nothing but the pink of sky and sea.

All the way home, in the front seat beside her father, she slept.

Bitter Wind

BARBARA GILMAN

THE SNOW was piled so high on either side of the walk
that Olivia Marvin, walking carefully on the sanded
parts of the pavement, imagined them walls of pure
white stone buttressing a legendary fortress. For a moment
she forgot the injustice of its being Saturday morning, a
day when she should be comfortably snoozing in bed instead of on her way to the weekly art class at the museum.

It took three quarters of an hour by subway and the
Huntington Avenue trolley to reach the museum, which
was why she had to leave the house almost as early as on
school mornings. Her mother was always telling her that
"getting adjusted" made hard things easier to bear as you
grew older; but Olivia sometimes wondered if her mother
hadn't forgotten how painful it was to be twelve and a
half.

A taxi horn shrilled. The driver stuck his head out of the
window and yelled, "Want to get killed, kid?"

Olivia jumped backward into the snowdrifts. She said, "Hell's bells," good and loud and, though warm tears pricked at the corners of her eyes, she felt better.

Inside the subway station, which smelled of wet wool and hot rubber, she dug around in her purse for a dime. She shoved the coin into the slot and ran clumsily toward the subway train just pulling into the station. Her thighs always seemed to get in the way of her moving swiftly, comfortably. She knew she was fat—her mother was always telling her to hold in her stomach—but inside Olivia felt as thin and graceful as Leslie Fanning. Leslie could go up the school stairs two and even three at a time, her legs were so long. She had the face of a young Medici prince, creamy-skinned, with a half-gentle, half-sullen mouth, and her brown hair, turned under at the edges, fell in thick wavy locks. Some day, Olivia thought, she would paint Leslie wearing a red velvet skullcap and call it "Portrait of Leslie Fanning." And Leslie would be proud of her artist friend.

At Park Street Olivia left the subway and walked up a flight of stairs behind a very fat old woman who wheezed and paused at every step. Olivia's feet felt too big. She wanted to push them under the old lady, like a lever, so that she could really hurry.

"Damn," she said under her breath. "Damn it to hell."

She knew her mother did not like her to swear, but it made her feel better all the same. Leslie Fanning said damn and hell all the time. The words covered up the raw feeling that struck Olivia whenever she had to walk into the school dining room alone, knowing that no one had saved a seat for her. Or when, as they were changing from their gym clothes, Leslie had said, pulling her soft cashmere sweater over her head, "Why do you wear that brown dress all the time, Olivia? Don't you have any others?"

"It's from a New York store," Olivia had mumbled.

But Leslie replied, "Why do you get your clothes in New York? Mummy says Clark's is just as good."

So, of course, Olivia could not tell her that the dress had been handed down to her from her cousin or that her mother was always saying in a voice which sounded almost noble, "Yes, Clark's has nice things, but we can't afford them."

Olivia realized that she lived according to a pattern that made a secondhand dress from New York better than the fancy satin blouses worn by thick-faced Katie Hoag. Even though she had to ride home in the subway from school, Olivia knew she was a "lady," while Katie Hoag, who was called for by a chauffeur, was "cheap." This was because she didn't say "real good" and "huh" the way Katie did. Also Olivia smelled of scented soap, not five-and-ten perfume.

Now the trolley was crawling up out of the tunnel, and because Olivia's feet were cold she put them on the hot pipe that ran under the seat before her. Soon they would pass the window of the steamship line on Boylston Street where there were posters of Blois, Notre Dame and the Riviera. Some day she would go back to Europe and live there, and paint. She remembered a little village deep in the mountains, where the streets were so narrow and dark that the houses almost met over the sidewalks. Sometimes, an archway connected two opposite houses, bridging the street.

"Sospel." She said the name of the village in a half-whisper to herself. It had a beautiful sound, and she was annoyed when the garlic-smelling man in the seat next to her turned and stared at her. Olivia smiled tolerantly at him. He didn't know he was sitting next to a future great artist. Some day he would see a picture of her in the paper, *Miss Olivia Marvin, native of Boston, winner of the Prix de Rome*. He would think: Why, that's the little girl I sat next to in the Huntington Avenue trolley one day. Imagine!

She was deep in her favorite pastime, murmuring the

words of her biography as they would someday appear in *Who's Who*. "Olivia Marvin was born in Cambridge, Massachusetts, daughter of a professor of ancient history at Harvard. At the age of ten, her parents took her on a trip to France and Italy, where she came to admire the works of the great French and Italian painters—particularly Botticelli and Puvis de Chavannes—whose influence can clearly be seen in her paintings. After graduating from the Winsor School in Boston, Miss Marvin entered Bryn Mawr College, which she left after two years to study at the Ecole des Beaux Arts in Paris."

The trolley stopped alongside a movie theater. Olivia stared at the huge gaudy posters flanking the entrance. She felt herself go a little hot in her stomach, for one picture showed a man kissing a woman's shoulder. She memorized the title of the movie so she could watch for its arrival at the University Theater. She hoped it would come on a Friday, when she got out of school early. Then she could go and see it before her mother returned from the symphony.

The trolley had rounded the curve beyond the Opera House. One more stop and then the museum. Olivia's feet were hot and sticky inside her galoshes. She walked to the door in the middle of the car, and as soon as the scarred orange doors slid open, she stepped off.

The classroom was in the basement. Big pipes twisted across the ceiling. The room was lighted by a row of windows along one wall, but since they faced south, the sun poured in all morning.

Olivia took a big pad, art gum, pencils and a paintbox from her locker and moved to her seat near the wall. Usually she sat with Mildred Hayes. Mildred Hayes was kind of dumb, but she went to the movies a lot and could always tell Olivia exactly what happened in them. She didn't draw very well and was always saying, "Gee, Ollie, you're wunnerful. You have such wunnerful ideas."

No one at school had ever called Olivia wonderful, but no one had ever called her Ollie, either. Besides, Mildred went to junior high and was unattractive, so her praise did not really count: it was virtually the same as being admired by Katie Hoag.

Olivia's mouth tightened in disapproval as she watched some of the big dark boys, who really frightened her, roughhousing at the end of the room. One of the girls stood near them, talking too loud and giggling too much. They didn't feel about drawing and painting as she did; she didn't see why Mr. Leavitt allowed them in his class.

"Hullo, Olivia, c'n I sit by you?" a quiet voice asked. Olivia jumped. For a moment she stared at Concetta Tagliarda's dark, big-eyed face and then at the raveled elbows of Concetta's sweater, where her middy sleeve showed.

"This seat is saved for Mildred," Olivia answered quickly.

"Oh." Concetta edged away. There was no doubt about it, Concetta smelled. And there were dark lines all around her fingernails, not just under the edges. Olivia knew that there were a lot of children like Concetta in the class, but she took care not to talk to them or sit next to them. Children like that were the reason she went to private school. She put up with them only because Mr. Leavitt was the best teacher and because she knew you had to do hard things if you were going to be famous.

Mr. Leavitt closed the door; class was about to begin. Mildred had not come and the seat beside Olivia was still empty. She saw Concetta standing by the door, pressing her pad and paintbox hard against her side. And now Mr. Leavitt was saying in a clear, chilly voice, so that (oh, agony) everyone in the class could hear, "Why don't you sit with Olivia Marvin, Concetta?"

Olivia pulled the edge of her brown skirt under her legs as Concetta slid into the neighboring seat. She was so close she could see the smear of chocolate in the folds of Concetta's shiny serge skirt. She could see the little gold chain, set with pieces of colored glass, against the dark flesh of Concetta's grubby neck.

"We're going to use free brush today," Mr. Leavitt was saying, "Fifteen minutes for each sketch. I'll assign the subject and you can go ahead from there. After that, we'll do life sketches while someone poses. The first subject is Wind."

The buzz of talk in the room gradually stilled. The sunlight from the window laid a bright hand across the rough white paper before her. Olivia twirled her paintbrush, hollowing the hard square of black pigment, thinking. She knew right away that she would paint Boreas, the north wind. She dipped her paintbrush into the black and began to paint. At first it was hard to make the brush move as she wished; she liked working with a pencil much better. The brush had a way of making broad lines where she wanted narrow ones. And she couldn't erase them either. She had to throw away several sheets before she got properly started. But after that, it was wonderful.

She was glad that Mildred was absent, for Mildred's chatter would have distracted her. She watched with satisfaction as her hand outlined the curve of the wind god's wings, and the ripple in his back-tossed hair. She wrapped him in a long billowing cloak because she loved to draw folds and besides, there were parts of a man's body that she could not draw. She didn't like to look at the male statues upstairs. The word *naked* leaped like a flame in her mind.

"Time!" called Mr. Leavitt. "The next subject is Water."

Olivia had never worked so hard. She was glad she had chosen to do Boreas first, because now she could do the other gods, and they all went together in a series. Fire was the next subject, then Earth.

Finally, Mr. Leavitt told the class to set the paintings in a row along the opposite wall so all the pupils could observe them from their seats at the worktables. The class talked and laughed as the paintings were being set up. Mr. Leavitt opened the door into the hall because the room was growing stuffy. Only Concetta said nothing. She hadn't even asked to borrow Olivia's rag to wipe her brush.

After a while she asked, "Do you like to paint?"

"Yes," said Olivia stiffly, almost fiercely. She wasn't going to let Concetta in on her private feelings. Fortunately, Mr. Leavitt now began to discuss the sketches. Olivia sighed with relief.

She didn't listen very carefully as he pointed out that the sailboat in the first picture was moving in the opposite direction to the waves. She was waiting until he began to talk about hers. He would say it was the only one in the group that showed real imagination, and then he would ask Olivia to explain about Boreas because, of course, the rest of the class didn't study mythology in public schools. Mr. Leavitt stopped at the sketch next to hers, and her heart was beating so heavily that she could scarcely hear what he said.

The picture showed a child standing on a street corner, her shoulders hunched up, a newspaper blown flat against her legs. A lock of hair swept a broad diagonal line across the lower part of the face, so that the top seemed just a pair of big dark eyes.

"Now what's good about this picture?" Mr. Leavitt asked.

One of the boys at the back of the room said, "Perspective."

"Yes, the perspective is well handled, she's got the angle of the street corner and the building just right. What else?"

"The proportions of the kid," said someone else.

"Yes," Mr. Leavitt said slowly. "What else?"

"It's a real kid." A girl's voice spoke eagerly. "I seen my little brudder stand onna street corner like that tons of times."

"Good," said Mr. Leavitt. "But nobody's hit on the right answer yet. Why does your little brother stand on the street corner, June? Why doesn't he play in the street?"

"Cause when the wind blows, it's warmer near a building, of course." The girl was bored now; she looked at Mr. Leavitt as if she thought he was dumb.

"Exactly," said Mr. Leavitt. "Now this is what I mean. This picture is the only one where the artist has *implied* the wind by showing what it does. There isn't any wind in the picture, actually, but you feel it, don't you? It's a cold sort of picture, isn't it? You know that child is cold."

"Oh sure," a lot of the children muttered.

"What this picture has, then, is feeling," Mr. Leavitt said. "It's what every really good picture requires. Otherwise, it's just a good-looking composition or an interesting one, like this—" He was at Olivia's picture now. "This is interesting because, instead of planning her composition on a straight line, this artist has planned it on the slant. It gives the drawing a sense of movement, and that's good. However, I don't think it's very clear." Mr. Leavitt bent down to examine the initials Olivia had printed in the lower left-hand corner. "Olivia Marvin," he said. "Suppose you tell us what this picture's about, Olivia. The subject I assigned was Wind. I don't see it here."

Words tangled in Olivia's throat. She found she could not make them emerge clearly, as she wanted to.

"It's Boreas, the north wind," she mumbled. "The Greek god Boreas, the north wind. It's a picture of him."

"Oh," said Mr. Leavitt. "I see. Well, let's go on to the next."

Olivia sat very still, stricken. He hadn't liked it. He hadn't said anything about imagination or intelligence. He hadn't talked about it nearly so much as he had about the picture of the child on the street corner. He had reached the end of the row, and Olivia watched him turn back to the middle. He stood and looked at both Concetta's and Olivia's pictures again, and then he said, "Concetta Tagliarda has done another very remarkable thing here. It's very interesting that her picture should be placed next to Olivia Marvin's, because they are at opposite poles. Concetta has interpreted Wind as she has seen and felt it *herself*. Olivia has used an idea—an interesting idea—but her work lacks the reality of Concetta's for just that reason."

Olivia turned and stared at Concetta, who was blushing and twisting the pleats of her dirty serge skirt. She was staring at the floor. She said nothing, as if she were ashamed of her picture.

Mr. Leavitt was dragging out a chair now. "It's your turn to pose today, Olivia," he said.

Olivia hated to pose. Sitting there, she felt fatter and lumpier than ever, but that wasn't why she suddenly wanted to hurry out of the room. She knew the other pupils didn't like her because she was much better than they were and she was going to be a great artist. Today, especially, she didn't want them to look at her—right after Mr. Leavitt had told them how much better Concetta's picture was than hers. She would say she was too tired to pose . . .

"Come on, Olivia, the class is waiting," said Mr. Leavitt. His glasses had slid down to the end of his thin pointed nose, so that Olivia could really see his eyes. They were a mild, cloudy blue and very kind. A lot of little red lines wiggled around the blue part. Then Mr. Leavitt smiled, and right away Olivia was sure that he knew she didn't want to pose. He almost seemed to be waiting for her to say, "I'm tired, do I have to?" And so she lifted her head, and moved forward, ready to fool him.

"How do you want me to pose?" she asked.

Mr. Leavitt made her sit with her back to the class, so that she was facing her own picture. The room was very quiet, and she could feel the pressure of the children's eyes on her shoulders.

She listened to Mr. Leavitt's soft voice as he walked

around the tables, criticizing. Her own eyes shifted from her picture to Concetta's and back again. Then they slid to where the coats hung opposite the lockers in the corridor beyond. The one on the end hook—it might have been Concetta's—was of faded red wool. The edge of the collar shone a little and so did the cuffs. Part of the lining had ripped; and it hung in a lopsided triangle below the hem. Beyond, Olivia could see her own coat, with the fuzz of the tweed so thick that it stood almost separate from the surface.

Olivia turned her eyes swiftly toward her own picture. "It's good, it's *good*," she repeated to herself, but her glance kept wavering back to Concetta's picture. Suddenly she shivered. How queer that she should grow cold just from looking at it, because the room was warm. And then, although she was staring at the picture, she could feel the sight of Concetta's coat pressing into the corner of her vision. The worn collar, the hanging hem, the sagging seams.

Concetta really knew what it was to be cold. Her picture was good because it made Olivia believe in a bitter wind that had never blown upon her. Olivia hadn't painted anything she felt—like Leslie, or the hand-me-down dress. She had painted Boreas, something she had only read about. Why, she didn't even believe in a wind god! She had painted Boreas only to show everyone in the class how much smarter she was than they.

"O.K., Olivia," Mr. Leavitt said. "That's all for today, class."

Her feet sand-heavy, her neck stiff, Olivia went back to her place. She reached for her open paintbox and closed it, for now it was time to go home. And she wondered, clouding the water with her paintbrush, whether she would come back here next week. She was aware of Concetta squeezing the left-over black paint from her paintbrush and closing her paintbox.

She spoke with great effort. "I think your picture is swell, Concetta."

"Thank you," Concetta murmured. Olivia looked at the sketch Concetta had made of her. "Do you like it, Olivia?" the girl asked.

"Yes—" Olivia said, a little uncertainly. She knew that the next thing she said would matter a great deal to Concetta, even though Concetta knew she would be a better artist than Olivia some day. "I think you made me look a lot thinner than I am," she said.

She put on her coat and walked upstairs, through the high galleries and through the museum doors into the abrupt winter sunlight. She looked across Huntington Avenue to a row of dingy brick houses. She noticed how the chimneys stuck up at different levels and how the big icicles hung down over the eaves in the same jagged way; how the lines of the trolley wires ran parallel to the line of the roofs and to the gray stripe of the sidewalk. Between the two lines moved the bright orange trolley.

Olivia thought, I must paint that next time; it's a good design. And then she ran eagerly beside Concetta to catch the trolley.

The Final Question

J. P. FOLLINSBEE

A TINY patch of sun began to invade the corner of Jennifer's desk. Its modest intrusion arrested her pen in its flight across the pages of the blue-covered examination book, and she glanced up, startled.

The tall Gothic windows of the high school were aglow, which meant that the afternoon had begun to lean into the west. There wasn't a great deal of time, then. Her watch confirmed it. Three-ten. In less than an hour she'd have to close the book, sign her name on the cover—and seal forever the fate of the scholarship and all it could mean. How the time had gone! Eight exams, and now she had less than an hour to complete the last . . .

Only one question left—one final question. *Composition IV. Section 12 (b). Write an essay of 700 words on any topic.*

It should be easy. Her mind attacked the problem. Essay,

she decided, was the key word. They didn't want a description, or a warmover of your summer vacation. You were expected to say something thoughtful, with significance and meaning.

The patch of sun moved teasingly onto the paper, and she found herself staring at it. How quiet the room was! Only the faint scratching of a pen, the whisper of a page turning, the scuffle of a foot.

She looked up, and the room was familiar; the leaning, writing figures around her were familiar. Yet everything was subtly changed. Everyone had withdrawn into a private orb of thoughts.

Impatiently, she pulled the book away from the distracting patch of sun. She mustn't let her mind drift. She frowned at the challenge of *Section 12 (b)*. Just this one last question and she could close the book and walk out into the clean, fresh day—a moth escaping forever the cocoon of Hilliston High.

But it was on this question—the last of all in the last exam of all—that the scholarship might depend. The words of the scholarship application leaped into her mind. *The Huntingdon Scholarship. Open to young woman demonstrating the required excellence of scholarship and leadership.* Jennifer couldn't help smiling. Even with its progressive reputation, Huntingdon clung to a mild, Victorian flavor. She turned to a clean page.

An essay of 700 words. It should be so easy. Her mind began to review the essayists she had studied. Ruskin, G. K. Chesterton, Ralph Waldo Emerson, Thoreau . . . any would serve as a model. But from somewhere the uneasiness of the past two weeks had come whispering back, filling her mind with a frightening emptiness.

Why couldn't she think? Not lifting her head, she stole a glance around the room. Was anyone else having trouble? Was Mark? No, he would be writing with utter concentration.

Glancing sideways she could see him bathed in sunlight, sitting by the window. The clean, strong planes of his face were composed and quiet. He was writing steadily. Of course! Nothing would ever disturb the even flow of his pen across the pages.

What had happened to her? A moment ago she had been writing without being aware of time or space. Then the patch of sun had come, and a doorway had opened in her mind.

She thought of the moment, two weeks ago, in Mape's drugstore. The moment when the first doubts had come. . . .

They had written their first exam that day—algebra. Afterwards, the gang had swarmed to Mape's for a post-mortem. She and Mark had pushed their way to a back booth through screams of "Wasn't it awful!" and "Well, one flunked—seven to go!" None of the chatter was real, of course. If it had been, there would have been only a gloomy silence.

Over a Coke, Mark had grinned at her. "Well," he'd asked. "How did it go?"

Until that moment, the scholarship had been just a frantic dream. She couldn't possibly win it. She would write for it, and then go to State, like everyone else. Like Mark, particularly. They would be together, and nothing would change at all. But sitting in the tiny booth, looking into his steady gray eyes, she admitted that unless she had made a mistake in simple arithmetic, her paper had been perfect. And like a shadow falling across all their plans, the scholarship had begun to edge into reality.

"All right, I think," she had smiled. "Fine. And you?"

"Fine." He had tossed the word back to her, and the exchange had been added to the long list of quiet understandings between them. "In fact, if the rest go as well, pre-med will be a cinch."

"And I may even make Huntingdon," she said lightly.

Mark had pushed his straw down into the ice floating in his glass. His face had become suddenly serious.

"I hope so, Jen. You deserve it, and it's what you wanted." Then he'd looked up and their eyes had caught. "Your special dream, remember?" He smiled. "Of course, it won't be the same at State with you not there."

She had tried to forget it, tried to concentrate on the exams that followed, certain that sooner or later one would catch her. If there was just one question that she honestly couldn't answer, all the hesitations and doubts would dissolve and vanish. She would have done her best, and she and Mark could go on making plans for State, together. But somehow the unanswerable question hadn't come.

"Are you having any difficulty, Jennifer?" a voice asked quietly.

Miss Simmons was smiling above her, solicitous and anxious. Poor Miss Simmons! It must be terrible to sit helplessly by and watch your students wrestle with the knowledge you had tried to give them. If they failed, she failed too—as a teacher. Jennifer smiled.

"No trouble," she whispered back. "Just thinking."

"I saw you stop." Miss Simmons smiled encouragingly. "It's three-fifteen." Her hand touched Jennifer lightly on the shoulder, and she glided off into the silence.

Three-fifteen! It seemed to echo through the room. She must decide. Quickly.

Decide. The word seemed to dance along the desk top and lose itself in the growing pool of sunlight. Decide what? She tried to push the idea back. But it wouldn't go back. It would be so easy. Just to close the book, and not answer the last question of all. The world wouldn't stop turning if you didn't go to Huntingdon. You didn't love Huntingdon. . . .

And after all, what was it? Just a stuffy, old-fashioned college for girls.

No, it was more than that. Its modest ivy-covered building sheltered the country's leading center for child study. Eminent professors—men and women whose names were respected all over the world—taught there. To be accepted by Huntingdon was an expensive privilege. To gain scholarship entrance, especially in child study, was a considerable honor.

Then why didn't she write? While there was still time. Minutes were ticking by. Minutes that could never be regained. She forced herself to stare at the words. *An essay of 700 words on any topic.*

Why had Mark said that in Mape's? In just that special way. *It won't be the same at State, with you not there.* And even before that. *Your special dream—remember?*

How could she forget? They'd been dating for about a month when she'd first told him of it. To the gang, they had already become Mark and Jen—like that, two names together. And it had already begun to seem natural, something intended to last.

That evening—it had been alive with October wind and rain—they had come racing home from the movies, and impulsively decided it was a night for popping corn in the fireplace.

Later, they'd talked of the future. She had told him, then, about her dream of going to Huntingdon. Of how her summer job at the play center had convinced her that her career lay in working with children.

"There are so many kids who don't get the breaks we've had, Mark," she'd said. "They need trained people to care about them and help them."

Mark had smiled. "You're a funny girl, Jen. One minute you're like a kid. And the next you're suddenly grown up. Things like Huntingdon are terribly important. You've got to be really sure you believe in them."

"I do." She'd smiled, too, and their hands had touched. "But Dad couldn't possibly afford to send me. It's a nice dream, that's all. Isn't there something you want more than anything, Mark? I think everyone needs one special dream."

"Mine isn't exactly a dream, Jen," he'd said quietly. "I'm going to be a surgeon. That's my dream, if you like."

Mark. Always so sure, so positive. She had admired his sureness then, but as the winter had worn itself out on the long succession of months, her feeling had become much more. Being with Mark gave the simplest things enchantment. They'd skated and skied and danced—even studied together. Somehow they had fallen in love, without saying it, without thinking of themselves as "going steady." It was deeper, more natural than that. And it hadn't mattered as much when her father had told her definitely that he'd only be able to send her to State. In a way, it had been a glad relief, because she and Mark belonged together.

Then, late in April, Miss Simmons had suggested that she try for the Huntingdon Scholarship.

"That's where you should go, Jennifer," Miss Simmons had said. "I'd like to recommend you for it. I think you would have an excellent chance."

It was a golden apple held tantalizingly just out of reach. Of course, she would try. She wouldn't reach it, but she would try. Everything else had been lost in the first breathless rush of excitement. Mark had been excited, too, and it had become a challenge for both of them. Neither had stopped to think, then, what it might mean to be separated. Huntingdon was only a hundred miles from State. They'd be together weekends and holidays.

Now it was nearly over. Jennifer looked down at her hands. Her fingers were stiff, tense. If only she could talk to someone for a minute. Or walk out under the trees and sky, where the close urgency of the room wouldn't smother her . . .

She was being foolish and melodramatic, of course. You had to make a decision. And you made it.

If she *did* finish, Mark would probably go on to State alone. Oh, they'd write—in the beginning. They might even spend a weekend together. Then Mark would hit his stride. State was famous for pretty girls. He'd have to study hard, but there'd be time for dates. And she would be a hundred miles away. He'd make new friends, and there wouldn't be time to write letters. . . .

They would move—not a hundred miles apart—but into two different worlds. Why hadn't she seen that in the beginning? He into the gay, social whirl of State; she into the quiet academic halls of Huntingdon, where a Sunday afternoon tea party was an event. Slowly their lives would drift apart.

She drew her pen hard across the blotter, leaving a fat, blue streak.

And if she decided not to finish. . . . ? She looked up at Mark's profile, the unfinished question mirrored in her eyes. He was writing calmly, without any apparent doubt at all. If only he would look toward her! If only he would smile! But he didn't turn.

The patch of sun had widened, until now the whole desk top shone with its warmth. *You've got to be really sure you believe.* Mark had said that. And it was true. You did have to believe. He didn't need to turn. All that he could say in this moment had been said in the long year they'd been together.

She moved her pen to the top of the page.

On Making Decisions, she wrote.

The words stood out, crisp and sure. She would probably lose Mark, now . . . But you couldn't hold onto something dear by deceiving yourself. That would be running away. Mark could never be proud of someone who didn't try. Even Shakespeare had said it, long ago. Perhaps written it down just for the sake of people who were confused. *"To thine own self be true. . . ."*

She smiled. Huntingdon wouldn't appreciate a borrowed epigram. Scholarship students were expected to think for themselves—with significance and meaning.

How could she best say it now?

At some moment in our lives, she wrote, *each one of us comes, like a traveler, to a crossroads without signs. Such crossroads, and they may be few or many, call upon decision. For each decision is a compass of our human happiness.*

The room began to fade. Her pen flew faster. . . .

Mark was waiting in the hallway. Everyone else had vanished. She had been the last to finish.

"How did it go?" he asked.

"Fine," she said. "And you?"

"Fine," he echoed, and they both laughed. "I was afraid you were going to be in there for life. Nothing went wrong, did it?"

She shook her head. "I had a little trouble with the last question," she admitted. "I lost a few minutes."

They started down the hollow, ringing stairs. How still the school was, Jennifer thought. As though it had sighed, and was settling into its summer's rest.

"Trouble?" Mark asked. "I thought essays were your specialty."

"Not this time. I—I wasn't quite sure what I wanted to say." It would be so easy to tell him. But she wouldn't, now. It was finished. She had found an answer to the final question in her own way.

He threw open the heavy door, and the sun was like a warm waterfall, drenching them in its abundance.

"It doesn't seem possible that it's all over," Mark said.

No, it doesn't seem possible, Jennifer thought. *All over!* It was such an unconsciously apt phrase. Not ended, not finished. Just—over. . . .

"You expect to feel glad," she said quietly. "You expect to want to run and race or do something foolish. But it's funny, I don't feel that way at all."

"Neither do I." They started down the cinder roadway to the gates. "Jen, let's not go to Mape's. Let's get our bikes and ride out to Wilson's Pond."

"All right. Wonderful!" she said.

He probably wanted to say good-by now, while they were both in a quiet mood that lent itself so perfectly to saying good-by. And it really was good-by, she realized with a shock. Mark was leaving Monday for a summer job in the mountains. It was funny how there was never any time—to finish a question, or to say good-by properly. . . .

The sandy road was packed firm with spring rains. They raced along it, not talking, to the edge of the pond.

Mark propped the bikes against a tree.

"Race you to the Big Rock," he said. And they ran.

The Big Rock was a tiny stone escarpment jutting out over the water. In summer it was a diving platform, in winter the place where skating fires burned. Now, it was quiet with spring.

For long minutes, they didn't speak. Then Mark idly skipped a fragment of stone across the still water, and the pond broke into a million ripples.

"Jen," he said. "I've been thinking. About us, I mean. If you win the Huntingdon, it'll mean you'll be up there four years, at least."

"That's right, Mark." What more could she say? She had to let him tell her in his own way.

He pulled his knees up to his chin and looked out over the pond.

"You'll make a lot of new friends. We both will, I suppose. And it'll be tough to get to see you. The train connections from State are awful. I checked them."

Why didn't he just say it? It wasn't necessary to make excuses, or to lead up to it gently.

"Yes, Mark." Her voice had become an uncertain whisper.

He turned to look at her. His eyes seemed dark and worried.

"Jen, I suppose it's foolish, considering we're both so young. But these past two weeks, I've had a feeling that if you go to Huntingdon, we'll probably drift apart, the way people do. I even hoped a couple of times you wouldn't win the scholarship." He snorted. "Male conceit and selfishness, I guess. Naturally, your work has to come—come first."

What was he trying to say? She had never seen him so uncertain, so unsure.

"So I just wanted to get it off my chest, Jen." He ran his hand through his hair. "To tell you that if you find someone else—well, that's O.K."

A wind riffled across the pond and shimmered the still surface into a million lights. Jennifer watched it come alive, unable to believe that this moment was real. That Mark was saying all the things she had wanted to say. *Mark was afraid of losing her!*

"Mark. Remember the night we popped corn? And you said how important it was to really believe? I thought about it this afternoon."

A fleeting grin tugged at the corners of his mouth.

"So did I," he said. "What did you decide, Jen?"

She looked down at the rough face of the Big Rock and ran her hand over its cool surface.

"The weekend train connections *are* terrible from State to Huntingdon, Mark. I looked them up, too." They would be able to talk about it now, as they had done. As they would go on doing, because it could never be any other way. A relationship based on honesty could only grow honestly. "But they're fine from Huntingdon to State."

The wind picked up the ripples of the pond and sent them against the rock. Mark's hand covered hers.

"You know, at first I didn't understand quite what you meant," he said. "But in the last two weeks, I have. About the special dream, Jen." He looked up at her, and the last doubt vanished. "I have one—now."